# The Reluctant Rancher

## Jolene Navarro

## LOVE INSPIRED
### INSPIRATIONAL ROMANCE

# LOVE INSPIRED®

## INSPIRATIONAL ROMANCE

ISBN-13: 978-1-335-59825-7

Recycling programs
for this product may
not exist in your area.

The Reluctant Rancher

For questions and comments about the quality of this book, please contact us at CustomerService@Harlequin.com.

Love Inspired
22 Adelaide St. West, 41st Floor
Toronto, Ontario M5H 4E3, Canada
www.LoveInspired.com

Printed in U.S.A.

## "So how did you end up living on the ranch?" Enzo asked.

"When I moved back to town over a year ago, I moved in with my mom, but I knew I needed my own place. Quickly. Your sister offered me one of the old homesteads to rent. It's small, but it's perfect for me."

"Ana asked what I thought about renting the house out yearly instead of a weekend rental. One was more money, and one was less hassle. I supported her either way. She told me she was going with the one that was easier for her to manage. She didn't tell me it was for you."

"Would you have said no?"

He shook his head. "It's just strange she didn't tell me."

She eyed his to-go bags. "You don't happen to have mac 'n' cheese in those, do you?"

He grinned then winked before turning the SUV onto the ranch. "Who would go to the Painted Dolphin and not get the mac 'n' cheese?"

That unexpected grin created a fluttering in her chest. *No. None of that.*

A seventh-generation Texan, **Jolene Navarro** fills her life with family, faith and life's beautiful messiness. She knows that as much as the world changes, people stay the same: vow-keepers and heartbreakers. Jolene married a vow-keeper who shows her holding hands never gets old. When not writing, Jolene teaches art to teens and hangs out with her own four almost-grown kids. Find Jolene on Facebook or her blog, jolenenavarrowriter.com.

## Books by Jolene Navarro

### Love Inspired

#### Lone Star Heritage

*Bound by a Secret*
*The Reluctant Rancher*

#### Cowboys of Diamondback Ranch

*The Texan's Secret Daughter*
*The Texan's Surprise Return*
*The Texan's Promise*
*The Texan's Unexpected Holiday*
*The Texan's Truth*
*Her Holiday Secret*
*Claiming Her Texas Family*

Visit the Author Profile page at LoveInspired.com for more titles.

The Lord thy God in the midst of thee is mighty;
he will save, he will rejoice over thee with joy;
he will rest in his love, he will joy over thee
with singing.
—*Zephaniah* 3:17

Thank you to Amy Beckman and other midwives providing holistic care and advocating for women's health.

# Chapter One

The smell of jasmine and the rhythmic beat of the rocking chair should have been calming, but Enzo Flores discovered he did not do calm very well. The rocker had been on this front porch for five generations. It was as solid as the family's heritage of love for the land. When he was younger, he'd thought the ranch gene had skipped him. He had wanted to go out into the world.

He stood and moved to the steps. This far from civilization, the Texas night sky glistened with endless crushed diamonds. He hoped that the ranching gene was just dormant, because he was going to need it for the next month or so.

Feet braced and arms crossed over his chest, he stared into the abyss for a moment then paced to the other end of the porch. It was too quiet. The silence couldn't be trusted.

He didn't belong here on a porch, in a rocker. He was an FBI special agent, but after the mess of his last mission, he'd been told by his director to take time off while the investigation was being done. He still wasn't sure what had gone wrong. Had his mistake put the rookie in the hospital fighting for his life?

With his hands braced on the railing, Enzo hung his head. His parents' call had been timed perfectly. A welcome distraction. They were in Peru, where they had been living for the last year doing missionary work. The project was an accumulation of several years of laying a foundation for a self-sustaining orphanage.

His mother had been in tears on the phone, and she didn't cry often. Her backbone was stamped from generations of Texas women who took charge and dealt with life while taking care of the people they loved. Her tears would always bring him to his knees.

Ana, his little sister, had been told to stay off her feet to protect her pregnancy. With her husband deployed and their parents in South America, Enzo was the only one left. His mother wanted him on the ranch to make sure his hardheaded sister didn't overdo it.

His twenty-eight-year-old sister needed a babysitter. He had done it for their whole childhood, so he'd play the bossy big brother one more time. Until their parents could get here anyway. Or until her husband was released from duty. Then Enzo would go back to Denver.

After being gone so lone, this old world was more foreign than he'd expected. He had driven straight through from Denver and had arrived four hours ago. Sighing, he rocked back on his heels. His family had never asked for his help before.

His skin pulled too tightly over his bones. He didn't belong here. He didn't know anything about running the ranch.

Worse, he was also tasked with keeping to his five-year-old nephew out of trouble. And on all accounts, that would not be an easy undertaking. He was a stranger to the boy. It was an opportunity to bond with his nephew. He wasn't going to have kids of his own, so it was time to step up and be the best *tío*. It wasn't like the poor kid had any better offers. Unfortunately for Lorenzo his uncle option was limited to Enzo.

He had to ensure his sister was benched and his unborn niece remained safe until his parents arrived. This was good. It would keep him from obsessing over that last mission.

Knowing his mother's strong faith, she would claim it was all orchestrated by God.

Enzo didn't put much stock in God caring about the daily running of their lives.

Back in Denver, he had been running twice a day just to get out of his apartment. Not having answers about the last job, and no current project or team, was the real problem. His mind needed to have a task. A goal he could plan out and attack.

Shifting his brainpower to this new role wasn't easy. If he wasn't an FBI agent, he didn't know who he was.

At the age of twelve, one of Enzo's classmates had brought his uncle in for career day. Enzo had known he'd wanted to do something big. His room had been full of the model airplanes and ships that would take him around the world one day. Joining the air force or navy had sounded like a grand adventure, but when Officer Diego Banderas had started talking about keeping the home front safe as an FBI agent, Enzo had known what he'd wanted to do with his life.

That day in Mrs. Green's class, he'd become hyper focused on one goal. Being hired by the Bureau. He'd done his research and lived and breathed the FBI. Ranch work was something he'd had to do when they'd needed an extra hand to move cattle or bring in hay.

At first, his parents had been disappointed

about his lack of interest in the ranch and tried to discourage his new dream. His grandfather had become his unlikely ally.

To this day, he had a clear image of the Sunday dinner where his father had lectured about his Texas heritage and the blood of the land that ran through his veins. His grandfather had cleared his throat, stopping all other conversations. The old rancher was a man of few words, but that day, he'd told the family that God had a purpose for each of them, and it wasn't for them to question Enzo's.

Enzo had experienced a moment of guilt at seeing the tears in his mother's eyes, but then she'd nodded, agreeing with her father. From that moment on, his parents had stopped trying to convince him his place was on the family ranch. Even though they hadn't understood him, every member of his family had supported his aspiration to go out and conquer the world.

And he had, until his divorce and the disastrous last mission. Gripping the rail, he looked to the sky for answers, but found none.

With a grunt, he rubbed his neck. *Come on, Enzo. Snap out of it.*

He had a nephew to get to know and a sister to protect. This moping was a waste of time. Raising his gaze, he focused on the silhouette created by the sliver of moon. It gave enough light to cultivate deep shadows.

Seriously, how did a man relax with the knowledge that all this peace and quiet was an illusion? Somewhere in the world there was trouble and someone needed help. His help.

Closing his eyes, he took in a deep breath and focused on the scents and sounds around him. Mockingbirds were calling out to each other. The breeze carried the salty air off the coast.

If he really focused, he could imagine the waves rolling across the sand just a few miles away. This was home.

He'd spent years dreaming up ways of escaping the ranch and the tiny coastal town of Port Del Mar, Texas, but growing up here had made him.

There was an new urgency to find that part of him he had lost before the darkness of the world snuffed him out.

What if it was too late? Was his mother's faith strong enough to bring him home? He could identify with the prodigal son, except it wasn't wealth he had lost. Enzo was emotionally and spiritually broken.

He had stopped talking to God long ago. Maybe this was as much about him centering himself as it was about taking care of his sister and his nephew through her high-risk pregnancy. His family seemed to so easily trust in God. Why was his faith so weak?

His sister was the epitome of strength. She had stayed on the ranch and taken over for their parents so he could go out and live his heart's desire. She needed him now, and he owed her.

He stopped and cleared his head. There was a new noise behind him. Pacing to the far corner of the porch, he investigated the night. Somewhere out there were barns and holding pens.

No. The noise had been closer.

There it was again at the back of the house. Stilling, he tilted his head and focused. Probably just a raccoon or opossum. A grunt came through the night.

A very human-sounding grunt. The door was being messed with. Someone was trying to break into the house. The house where his sister and nephew slept.

Back against the wall, he silently moved from the front porch and eased his way to the back door. He paused and listened. There was mumbling, low and incoherent. Maybe a druggie looking for an easy mark?

There seemed to be only one intruder, and they were at the screened porch door to the kitchen. Moving closer, he could make out a lone person in the darkness. They were smaller than him, and it looked as if they had a box under one arm while they wrestled with the door.

Were they just going in to grab and go, or was there a target? Everyone in town thought his sister was on the ranch alone. No one was aware of his arrival.

He was close now, and the deviant was oblivious to his presence. With a quick move, he had the man in a chokehold. But it wasn't a man. The box dropped and soft hands came up to his arm.

This close, he could make out the person's features. Soft curved features. Wild hair refusing to be tamed by braids. In shock, he froze. It was Teresa Espinoza, his sister's best friend. Catching him off guard, she twisted around and hooked her leg behind his knee, knocking him off-balance.

"Resa, it's me. Enzo." They were already going down as he released her.

With a thud, they landed on their backs side by side. The thick St. Augustine grass softened the fall. For a solid minute, they lay there looking up at the night sky, both out of breath.

"Why did you try to kill me?" One hand on her head, she swatted him on his shoulder with her other. "My…my heart is racing a hundred miles a minute."

"Why are you breaking into the house? I could have injured you." Angry that she had put herself in danger, his words were sharper than intended. He had meant to apologize. Standing, he swiped at the grass on his slacks.

"I have a key, but it was sticking. I have no idea if it has ever been used. When did you get home?" She sat up, crossing her arms over her bent knees. "You nearly gave me a heart attack. Shouldn't you have called out and given me some kind of warning?"

"Why would I warn a burglar that I'm about to grab them? It defeats the purpose of a sneak attack. Why are you lurking around in the dead of night trying to get into my sister's house?"

With a frustrated growl, she plopped down again in the grass. "You are the most aggravating man I know. And believe me, I know a bunch."

"How does being logical make me aggravating? You're the one with questionable actions here. Really, it's two o'clock in the morning. What possible reason do you have for breaking into the ranch house?" He offered her his hand to help her up.

"I wasn't breaking…" With another disgruntled sound, she took his hand. The skin was soft and warm, but her grip was firm. "That door is never locked. You locked it, didn't you?"

On her feet, she quickly broke contact. Hands on her hips, he was reminded of the time she'd knocked him off the monkey bars at school for some forgotten offense. No one had believed him when he'd told the story of her getting mad at him and pushing him. They'd all just seen the sweet, easy-to-get-along-with Resa. He was the only one to have ever witnessed that side of her.

He crossed his arms over his chest. "In the wee hours of morning, you're trying to get into a house that is not yours. What would you call it?"

"Wee? When did you start talking like that." She rolled her eyes when he just stared at her. "I'm in charge of creating a special moment. Tomorrow... Well, today, I guess, is Ana and Julian's ninth anniversary. Julian asked if I could make sure to set up a surprise in the kitchen for when she walks in for her morning tea. They have a tradition of him fixing breakfast and giving her a gift first thing in the morning. With him being deployed right now, it's tough on them both. He's trying his best to keep things as normal as he can through me. What are you doing here?"

Enzo closed his eyes and dropped his head. "I'm sorry." Julian was a good man, better than him.

The apology came out easy enough, and nothing inside him combusted. That was good. "Julian *and* my parents asked if I'd come home and take over the running the ranch and keeping track of an active five-year-old while Ana is on bedrest. Apparently, my nephew is a ball of energy that needs a lot of attention, and they don't want her worrying about the daily operations of the ranch. So, I'm here to take care of everything until they can get back." He glanced at the now-crushed box on the ground. "What can I do to help with this?"

Tall and stiff, Enzo's dark hair was still perfect even after their tumble. Hers had to be a mess. His hard jaw was more chiseled than she remembered.

What was clear in her memories was the disapproving look.

When she had turned thirteen, she had become all too aware of him. He had been her first crush. She had worked so hard to get his attention, but the only time he noticed her was when his sister got in trouble. Every time, he blamed Resa.

All those teenage emotions had to be dealt with so she had become relentless. She blinked.

He just apologized. *To her.* It took the starch out of Resa's righteous anger. She lowered her arms and went over to the box dropped during the scuffle. She frowned. It didn't even qualify as a scuffle. She'd never had a chance. The only reason she'd gotten a move in at all was that he'd realized who she was and let his guard down.

In one fluid motion, he had picked up the box and was holding it out to her. "I'll install some motion-sensitive security lights. They have them at the barn. I don't know why Dad never put them around the house."

"It's to scare off four-legged predators. It's Port Del Mar. Doors are left unlocked," she said.

"I locked all the doors. And there is no such thing as a completely safe place."

Enzo had always been too serious for his own good, but as she looked in his eyes, she saw a darkness that wasn't there before. His parents were very proud of the work he did for the government. They didn't have all the details, but they knew he had worked hard to earn a spot with the Hostage Rescue Team. She was sure he used his master's in psychology to deal with hostage situations. Even as a kid, he had been super cool and steady, no matter what kind of chaos was going on around him. Chaos that had usually included his sister and her.

She imagined he was exceptional at what he did, but just like in her career as a midwife, no matter what you did, sometimes it could go wrong. Some things were just out of human control.

She picked up the items that had fallen out of her box. The carton itself was crushed on one side. There was only one survivor inside, but the marbled Bundt cake from Pan Dulce, her sisters' bakery, was no longer round.

"Doesn't look good." Enzo joined her with a broken teacup and a squished box of specialty teas. A bouquet of large sunflowers was tucked under his arm—petals missing and stems broken. It was a sad arrangement. "I can go into town first thing and get more sunflowers."

"Oh no. I'll make these work. Julian wants them in the kitchen as soon as she walks in for her morning tea." She took the flowers and handed the box back to him. "If you could put all that in there, I'd appreciate it. I don't see the gift."

With a sigh, she quickly scanned the area. "There's a wrapped gift box missing. It's yellow with a blue ribbon. It's a bracelet. And there's a white wicker basket. Everything was supposed to go into the basket." A little whine crept into her voice. *No time for that.* Boosting her attitude up a notch, she shook off the frustration.

Enzo was carefully organizing the items in the box.

"Thank you," she managed to say.

With a nod, he turned his phone into a flashlight. "My guess would be that they've rolled under the porch." He pointed out the likely path.

"Of course. Where else would they go?" She hated small dark spaces. Going to her hands and knees, she lowered her head, hoping to see them close to the edge.

Enzo joined her. "Here, let me. Are you still afraid of dark places?"

"Only when I can't see and it's coated in spider webs and has any sort of crawly creature. We've made an agreement. I stay out of their homes and they stay out of my sight. It's worked so far."

With a chuckle as if he found her amusing, he scooted past her and studied the ground. "From the angle the box fell, they probably rolled under the steps."

The back porch light came on, blinding her for a moment.

"Enzo? Is that you?" Holding the screen door

open, Ana stood on the top step, looking out into the darkness.

Resa stood. Enzo was under the steps now.

"Yes, and me," she answered.

Ana's eyes went wide. "Resa? What are you doing out here in the dark with my brother in the middle of the night? And where *is* Enzo?"

"Uh. He's under the house."

Enzo crawled out backward.

"What? Why? I don't understand. What is going on?"

He stood. "You are supposed to be in bed. Off your feet. Why are you out here in the middle of the night?" His voice had an edge to it that was reflected in his obsidian gaze.

His sister rolled her eyes. "My mouth was dry, so I went to get a drink. I heard something."

"And your response was to come outside by yourself?" He handed the basket with a wrapped box to Resa as he walked toward his sister. "And what were you going to do if it was something dangerous?"

With a puff of air, Ana put her hands on her hips. "I figured it was you out here. Who else would it be? I didn't know why you were outside, though. I thought you might need help or at the very least some light." She turned to Resa, her face scrunched in confusion. "Why are you out here in the dark with Enzo? I wouldn't be surprised at him doing some sort of nighttime security perimeter thing, but what are you doing?"

"If you go into the kitchen and sit down, I'll come tell you. Enzo is right about one thing. You don't need to be standing out here. Go sit down. We'll be right there."

With an exasperated sigh, Ana let the screen door slam behind her as she crossed the porch and went into the kitchen.

"That hurt, didn't it?" Humor danced along Enzo's words.

"What?" She picked up the box from the ground.

"Admitting I was right. To verbally say you agree with me." He chuckled. "That had to cause some sort of internal hemorrhaging."

"Ha. Ha. The Tin Man has jokes." She handed him the box.

"That nickname isn't any funnier now than it was when we were in school." His tone was as dry as West Texas.

"There are several people that think I'm funny." Giving him a hard time had been the only way she knew to get over him. She needed more fun in her life anyway. "Come on. Let's go wish your sister a happy anniversary while her husband is somewhere overseas saving the world. You superhero guys like to make life difficult for the rest of us."

"Did you just call me a superhero?"

She could hear his grin as she stomped up the two steps and squeezed past him. "You're more of a Spock kind of hero. All logical and boring. Give me Captain Kirk any day."

She grimaced at her own words. *Not anymore.* That lesson was learned. She'd earned her diploma. No more falling for all charm and no commitment. The plan was to get a family of her own. The traditional, boring kind. A husband with a nine-to-five job, a few kids and a couple of dogs.

An image of her cat, Princess Leia, curled up on her shoulder while they watched TV flashed in her mind. She had loved that cat, and it was too painful to think of replacing her with another one.

Princess Leia couldn't be replaced. That was one of Resa's problems. When she loved, she did it so completely and deeply that it was hard for her to move on even when it became obvious that it was the right thing to do.

But she was going to move forward and into her best life. With the help of Ana and her sisters, they were going to find her the perfect man so she could start the family of her heart.

The women had even gotten together and made a list for her. She just had to stick to it.

"Resa?" Enzo's voice cut through her thoughts.

"Oh…sorry. It's been a really long day. Come on. Let's give Ana her anniversary surprise."

Resa's unfortunate habit of investing in the wrong men was about to change. There was a plan in place. If she stayed on track, her lifelong dream of being a wife and mother would become a reality.

God had placed this desire in her heart long ago but then doubt had crept in. What if having a family wasn't in God's plan for her? Was she wanting something that might be beyond her reach? Maybe her purpose was helping others build their families?

Adoption was a good option for her. With a sigh, she followed Enzo into the old ranch house kitchen. She'd given herself a year. If she didn't connect with the perfect man, she'd move on to plan B.

Not that Ana and her sisters had allowed for plan B. They claimed it was admitting defeat before giving plan A any sort of chance.

Margarita, her oldest sister, had the whole package with an adoring husband and three kids. Josefina had her daughter. Even her baby sister, Savannah, who had claimed she'd never want to have kids, was off with her new family.

Of course, Ana had the husband of her dreams and was now adding baby number two. Not that it had been easy for her friend. The man she loved was in an undisclosed location for an undetermined amount of time, and this pregnancy was not going smoothly.

Trying to solve the problems of Resa's love life helped her friend not worry about her own problems. That was Resa's mission right now. To reduce the stress and eliminate useless worry from Ana's life so they could welcome a healthy little girl into the world.

Inside, Ana sat at the table scowling at her brother. Enzo was ignoring her as he blocked her view of the box. He shot a look at Resa, clearly blaming her for this whole mess.

Just like old times.

## Chapter Two

How was he going to fix this? The large homey family kitchen offered no answers. Ana needed to go to bed so Resa could set up the surprise. "We're safe in the house now. You should go to bed." Enzo stifled a groan and tried to smile as if he had not just accidentally challenged his sister to stay up all night.

"Enzo Remington Flores. Neither one of you have explained why you were outside under the house." Her eyes went wide. "Is there an infestation you haven't told me about?" Her gaze went to the floor and she scanned for any evidence of a problem.

Resa laughed and went to the table. "No. I just got in from a late night and wanted to drop off some—" she waved her hand in the air "—things I got for you."

He rolled his eyes. Really? That was the best she could do?

Ana raised an eyebrow and stared him down.

"What?" He winced. That was a very unpleasant high-pitched sound coming from his throat. How was it that he could keep his cool in any situation, but the minute his mother or sister gave him that look, he broke? He swallowed and glanced back at the box.

Ana tilted her head as her gaze bounced between Resa and him. She crossed her arms over her belly and leaned back. Her attention went to the box and the abused sunflowers, and her jaw went slack. "My anniversary." Tears welled up in her eyes.

*No. No. No.* He moved to the table but hesitated, not sure what to do.

Her shaking hand went to her heart. "Jules had you bring me our anniversary breakfast, didn't he?" Falling forward onto the table, his tougher-than-nails sister cried in earnest.

Resa rushed over and dropped to her haunches beside his sister. "Ana. It's okay. Julian loves you and he wants you to remember that."

Ana lifted her face and he saw that red tinged her eyes and splotches covered her cheeks.

"I know," she said. "I just miss him."

There was a red kettle on the stove, so he put water in it and set the flames high. "Do you want hot chocolate?" That had been her go-to when she was upset as a kid.

"Tea would be nice. Thank you, Enzo." She reached her hand across the table and wiggled her fingers at him. "Come over here. Sit with me."

The ladder-backed chairs were the same from his childhood. Sitting across from her, he took her outstretched fingers and gently squeezed them. "I might not have been around much, but you know I'll always come when you need me."

"I'm so glad you're home. You should have come earlier. It couldn't have been easy going through the divorce alone. How are you doing?"

He looked down. They didn't know he had waited months to tell them. Like six or eight. How sad was it that they hadn't noticed his wife had left him?

He had left home to do great things in the world. As soon as he was hired as an FBI agent, all his attention had focused on becoming a special agent and earning a spot on the Hostage Rescue Team. Six years ago, he'd accomplished that goal. But his mom was worried about him. Somewhere in his brain he had thought marriage was the next step and it would fill any remaining holes and make his parents happy.

Unfortunately, he hadn't known how to make a wife happy. His father and Julian made it look easy.

He hadn't been able to face the personal failure.

With a casual shrug, he made sure to give her an easy, relaxed smile. The one that he counted on to put people at ease. "It's done and in the past. There was a big case I was working on and… Well, there wasn't anything to be done. It was over, and we moved on."

He glanced at Resa and then looked away. He didn't want to talk about this, especially in front of her. It would only reinforce her belief that he didn't have a heart.

A part of him suspected she was onto something. Who gets married because it was the right time? Another box to check off. Everyone in his family married. He sighed. Only, they'd all stayed married.

To his detriment, he'd ignored the fact that the divorce rate in the FBI was 70 percent. His family had always asked about his girlfriend and when they would make it official.

He had dated Brittany on and off since college, and she'd left big hints that it was time to make the next move in life. She'd always been agreeable and never made demands on his time.

"Enzo?" Ana was leaning forward. "Talk to me. There was no way your marriage ended without some major damage to your heart."

He quirked an eyebrow. "That sounds overly dramatic. It happens. In the FBI, it happens even more. I shouldn't have gotten married."

"She seemed so sweet. I mean, we really didn't get to know her that well. Y'all didn't seem to ever disagree on anything."

"We never fought. She agreed with whatever I said."

A suspicious sound that could have been a snort came from his sister's best friend.

"Turns out she didn't really agree with me, she just didn't like conflict. She changed her mind about wanting kids, and I can't imagine bringing kids into the world I live in. It's a hard one to get over. While I was traveling, she found someone that wants the same things she does."

His dedication to the Bureau hadn't left him time to build a real marriage. A few months after the wedding, Brit had started pushing for kids. He had told her he didn't want children from the start. Foolishly, he'd thought the discussion was done. She'd admitted later that she had hoped he'd change his mind once they were married.

He'd come home a few days early and found

her on the couch with her *friend* Robert. What a cliché. At least they had just been cuddling and watching TV. When he'd asked what was going on, he'd been ready for her tears and excuses.

Instead, she'd jumped into offensive mode and attacked him. It was the closest thing they'd ever had to a fight. Robert stood close to her as if to protect her.

The quiet woman who had never shouted before had screamed at him. She'd complained that he'd never taken her anywhere, not even to the ranch to meet his family. Her finger had pushed at his chest with every point she'd made.

No calls. No email. She had yelled. They didn't go out to dinner. They didn't have friends. No kids. When he was traveling the world, she was stuck in their apartment, lonely. She'd thought he would be different after they were married.

Reeling from the unexpected attack, he'd just stood there. She'd taken the hand of the red-faced man standing next to her and told Enzo she needed more from a marriage than an empty house.

They'd stood in silence. There'd been no arguing about anything she'd said. It was all true. But he had thought she was happy. The betrayal had hit him hard. Why hadn't she said any of this when he'd been home?

Maybe he could have made changes if she had told him. But then again, as her husband, he should have seen it. It wasn't clear who he was angrier with, her or himself.

He looked away from his sister and stared through the archway into the family room. The soft neutral colors with pops of red and yellow pillows invited people to sit and talk, to hang out. Growing up his parents had spent so much time together in that room with friends and family.

The saddest realization had been the lack of emotion he'd felt when he'd come home after his next assignment and been served divorce papers.

"Marrying Brittany was selfish on my part. I was clueless and hurt a really sweet woman without meaning to. She's happy now, and I get to focus on my work."

Resa had moved away to make the tea. This discussion would only reinforce her opinion about him being cold and emotionless. Her opinion of him didn't matter, so why was he worried about it?

Ana shook her head. "I'm not buying it. You hate any type of failure. You loved her and she—"

"I know what she did." His voice was sharper than intended, but he didn't want to talk about it. Not then and not now. Especially not in front of Resa.

What did they want? For him to pour out all the hurt and cry over his injured feelings? Waste of time and energy.

"Sorry. It's just that Mom's so worried about you."

When he had finally gotten brave enough to call home and tell them the news, his mother had cried. Disappointing her had hurt more than his wife's leaving. *What was wrong with him?*

Resa joined them with three delicate cups of tea. She glanced at him then quickly averted her gaze. Half of her dark curls had escaped the long braid. He didn't remember her being so pretty in a wild sort of way. He sighed and took the cup from her soft fingers.

No clue what to say now, he took a sip. He pulled back and then went in for another. The flavor woke his taste buds. This was good. There was a bit of sweetness, citrus, and something he couldn't identify. "What is this?"

"Resa blends her own tea. This one is probably to help calm me." She smiled at her friend and Resa winked back at her.

"Did you and Brittany try counseling? If

not together then at least for yourself?" Ana was persistent.

"Shouldn't you be back in bed?" He looked to Resa for help.

"I can't set up your surprise until you go back to sleep. Finish your tea." Resa grinned.

"Fine, I'll finish my tea like a good girl." She smiled at her friend and then turned to him. "I get it, Enzo, it's hard to talk about, but bottling it up won't help." Eyes closed, she took a slow sip from the elegant cup covered in pink roses.

When her eyes opened, she narrowed her gaze at him. There was a new glint he didn't trust. When he had told her he was coming to the ranch to help, she had laughed.

She didn't believe he could handle the ranch.

"Did you get a chance to go over the list I gave you?" she asked.

He gave her a nod.

"Are you sure? Calibrations on the moisture meters for the hay need to be done tomorrow. Are you sure you know how to do the alignment checks to the irrigation system? I know it's been a while since you were on the ranch, so don't hesitate to ask for help. Resa is a valuable resource. She lives in the old homestead. She's helped with deworming the yearlings before also."

*She lives on the ranch?*

He was grateful for his training. His reactions never showed on his face. "Is it livable?"

Ana rolled her eyes. "No. She lives with raccoons and uses fire to cook. Of course, it's livable. Mom and Pops refurbished it about five years ago to rent to tourists, but with them and Julian out of the country, I didn't want to deal with the weekend renters, so I offered it to Resa. I can go with you tomorrow to meet our ranch hands, Seth and Brady. They're new."

His sister had been acting as the ranch manager for almost two years now. Their parents had wanted to take a more hands-on approach at the orphanage in Peru after several years of financially supporting the mission. Eight months ago, they'd signed up to live on the property for a year.

He pressed his lips into a tight line. Somehow, he had to convince her he could do this, otherwise, she'd be out of the house running the ranch. The goal was to never let her suspect he was out of his element and clueless.

"I'm more than capable of introducing myself to new people. I grew up here. I can manage a few weeks without destroying everything you've done."

He smiled. There was no way he was going to allow her to stress over the ranch. She didn't need to know he had no clue what he was doing. He was capable enough to figure it out. "Any word if Dad and Mom have found someone to take over for them?"

"No. You know Mom. She says it's in God's hands, and His timing isn't ours."

He nodded. The sooner his parents returned to the ranch, the better. He still didn't feel like he belonged here, but for the next few weeks or so, it was his turn to support their dreams and take care of things.

That's what *la familia* did. His dad's parents had taught him that. They'd come to the United States as a newly married couple to give their children a chance at education and a better life. They'd visited the ranch often when he was growing up. He had taken the support of his family for granted.

Now his sister's wellness and the health of his unborn niece was his priority. Once they were safe or in the hands of his mom, he would go back to fighting the bad guys.

Resa reached over and patted Ana's hand. "We are all here to help you." She turned to him. "Hey, remember, I grew up helping my dad on the ranch he managed. If she is pushing the limits and not listening to you, I'm on the other side of the driveway. I'm a call or shout away."

With an overly dramatic sigh, Ana dropped her shoulders and looked to the ceiling. "Really, people. I feel fine. I can still help. I promise not to get on a horse or lift bags of feed, but I don't expect you to do everything, Enzo. I mean you hated the ranch growing up."

"I didn't hate it. I just wanted to do something else, and I did. I've got this, Ana. Trust me. It's also a great time for me to get to know Lorenzo better. There is a chance I need to be here as much as you need to rest. Let me do this for you."

"Aw. See, Resa. I told you my brother has everyone fooled." She looked at him with that suspicious glimmer in her eyes again.

"No crying on the ranch. Wasn't that Mama Boo's number one rule?" he asked, hoping to distract her with their great-grandmother.

She laughed and rubbed her eyes. "Yes. But I don't know if that counts for pregnant cowgirls."

Resa gathered the empty cups and stood. "Enzo is home, and I'm here. We've got this covered. You aren't going to be worrying about the ranch or anything else. Relaxing and focusing on your new baby girl is your only job now." She moved to the sink and washed the cups.

"I don't know. Enzo hasn't been on the ranch

in years, and when he was here, he did everything to avoid working. He doesn't know Lorenzo, who can be a handful. And you have your job and a list of your own. I'm not going to allow you to use me as an excuse to not get out there and live your life. You have a future to find. I should be able to go to the barns and check things out." Blowing out a puff of air, she leaned back and looked at them. "I don't have to actually stay in bed twenty-four seven."

Drying the cups, Resa turned around. "I can spend my time however I see fit. I'm happy. My personal life is fine. My future is not going to be fixed in a week."

Ana shook her head and laid a hand on Enzo's arm. "She wants to get married, so her sisters and I made a list for her." She gasped and her eyes went wide. "You can help with that."

He frowned.

"No." Resa stood with her hands on her hips. "I've had enough help. I'm sure Enzo doesn't want any part of my dating life."

Leaning forward with excitement, Ana ignored Resa and looked straight at Enzo. "We've made up a list of men for her to date. All possible husbands. You can do background checks on the guys we don't know as well."

"No. I can't." What was going on? He didn't

like the direction of this conversation. "Seriously, Ana. You need to go to bed."

"Why can't you do the checks for us? The FBI can find out anything about anyone."

"It's illegal to perform a background check without cause. I can't just go around randomly doing checks on innocent people."

"What if they are pretending to be innocent?"

"No." And the thought of a husband list for Resa bothered him on too many levels.

Rolling her eyes, his sister shook her head. "You're no fun. I forgot what a killjoy you can be." She stood. "If anything goes wrong with Resa's list, it will be your fault." She yawned. "I'm going to bed so you can set up my surprise. Love you both."

She kissed him on the side of his head. He moved to stand to help her, but she waved him off. "Help Resa. She probably has to be at work early in the morning, and you have a lot to learn before I let you step foot in any of my barns or pastures. So it will be an early morning for you too." Wrapping her robe tighter around her, Ana shuffled out of the kitchen and down the hall to the library where her new easy-to-reach bed had been set up.

"Well, that could have gone better." Resa moved away from him and set the box on the table. She carefully inspected each item as she pulled it out.

"Sorry about the background checks. Really, it's a serious—"

"Don't worry about it. I would never expect you to do that."

She cut the stems of the three surviving sunflowers and put them in a small mason jar. "Helping me gives her something else to think about. Not being hands-on with the ranch is going to exasperate her. Being told to sit still is her nightmare."

He chuckled. "Yeah. Mom always said she rushed into the world early and never slowed down." He studied her profile. Why wasn't she married by now, with a handful of kids if that's what she wanted? "Who are the guys? Maybe I know them. You can also do a basic google search on your own. I'd ask friends and relatives. Actually, relatives are usually your best angle. If you can get an aunt or cousin talking, you can find out all sorts of interesting information."

He took the specialty tea bags from the squished box, cleaned off the grass, and organized them in the basket.

"You might know a few of them. I agreed to some of the dates to get my sisters and Ana off my back." She arranged the flowers and basket in the center of the table with the gift box in front.

Maybe he should have sent notes and gifts to Brittany when he was traveling. Too late now. "Are there any real contenders?"

"There is one or two that might be promising." Pulling out the damaged cake, she smiled and looked up at him. There was a new light shimmer in her eyes. A strange tightness hit his chest. Unruly wisps of hair danced around her face with pieces of grass trapped in the dark glossy strands. Impossibly long lashes emphasized eyes that made him think of polished tiger's-eye and the forest floor after a spring rain.

There had always been something untamed about her, but he'd never noticed how pretty she was. When had his little sister's best friend turned into a beautiful woman?

He shook his head and stood. Nope, not helpful thoughts. This whole experience was unsettling.

"My first date is the brother-in-law of one of the nurses at our clinic."

He watched as she cut a few perfect slices of cake with a very sharp knife and deliberate efficiency. Realizing she was still talking and he hadn't been paying attention, he blinked and tried to concentrate. Being home was messing with his mind. He scanned the kitchen for something to do.

"Enzo? Are you okay? Do you know Steve? He just moved to town, but I think he lived in Denver for a while." Concern filled her those brown eyes. Yes, they were just brown eyes. Nothing to be all poetic about.

Apparently, she had told him the man's full name already. "No. I don't know him." Probably not, anyway. He knew a couple of Steves, but they were too old and married. "I was just thinking about all the…um, stuff that needs to be done tomorrow. Ana gave me a list." Did that sound as weak to her as it did to him?

With a laugh, she clasped her hands together. "I'm so sorry. I'm sure the details of my love life bore you."

The skin behind his ear itched. Great, now he'd insulted her. "I was thinking how much Ana likes her lists. One for you. One for me."

"Ana does love her lists. I've always loved being spontaneous, but that has been to the detriment of my life goals. So, now I have a list. Steve Harper is promising. I mean this is a small town, and the dating pool is pretty shallow." She took the lopsided part of the cake to the counter.

"You want to stay in Port Del Mar?"

"I do. I left for a while, but being back with

my family feels right. I want to raise my kids here. What about you?"

"Me? I learned my lesson. One divorce is enough. Ana's doing a great job with the family heritage, and she'll pass it on to her kids."

She nodded as if she understood, but the light in her eyes was gone.

He straightened the chairs on his side of the table. "Ana is right about one thing. The morning will be here soon. Thank you for everything you've done for her."

"She's my best friend. If you need any help, just ask. If I don't know or can't do it, I will find someone in town that can. The goal is to keep her from stressing as much as possible."

"I've got this. Don't worry. Enjoy your dates. I hope you find your dream husband."

She eyeballed the ceiling. "That doesn't sound right. You have a good night's rest. Ana is going to be working you hard." She looked down at the crumbled cake. "I hate wasting this. It looks a little rough, but it's good. Would you eat it?"

"Crumb cake. Looks like a perfect breakfast for my nephew and me to start our day."

She gently opened the door.

He followed her to the porch, watching as she crossed the drive and went down the path that led to the one-room cottage built by his ancestors over a hundred years ago. The porch light was on.

He waited until she was inside before retreating into the ranch house and locking the doors. She probably hadn't locked her place.

Worrying about her was not his job. Tomorrow, he'd figure out what the ranch needed, and he'd get to know his nephew.

He'd take Lorenzo out with him. They could ride over the west pasture. He had plenty to do, and thinking about Resa Espinoza was not on the list.

# Chapter Three

Resa sighed and settled into her seat. She loved the Painted Dolphin. It sat on the pier with the garage-door like windows pulled all the way up tonight.

Date number one with Steve Harper was in progress. From their table, they could watch the boats sail by as the sun set. She remembered how Enzo had loved sailing as a kid. It was the only time she had seen him relax at all. Did he still sail? He didn't seem to do anything relaxing.

*No thoughts of Enzo tonight.* She turned and smiled at her dinner date. Steve had insisted on picking her up at her house. He had arrived with flowers.

Reaching for another of her favorite cheddar biscuits, she smiled at him. His shaggy blond hair wrestled the breeze and he kept pushing it back. He looked very relaxed in the Hawaiian-style button-down.

"Emma said you're enjoying our little beach town." Emma, one of the nurses at the clinic, had become a fast friend. When she'd heard about Resa's list, she had wanted to help. She'd offered her brother-in-law. He was new to Port Del Mar, so that was a plus. Resa had known most of the men in town for her entire life. Her search for a husband had become a community effort.

Steve nodded "So you grew up here?" he asked after their waitress left.

"I did." With a smile, she turned to absorb the ocean view. She tried not to be disappointed in the lack of a spark, but she was being logical now. Emma had promised that Steve was looking to get married and start a family. She needed to give him a chance and stop thinking of Enzo.

Why was her mind even going there? She shook her head and smiled at the man sitting across from her. This was her coworker's brother-in-law. He deserved her full attention.

Resa admired Emma and Thomas's marriage. So if his brother was anything like him, she had to keep an open mind.

The owner of the Painted Dolphin, Elijah De La Rosa, walked up to their table. "Resa!" He put a hand on her shoulder and gave her a gentle squeeze. "So happy to see you here. I had to stop by and thank you for working Jazmine into your schedule." He turned to Steve and shook his hand.

Resa introduced them and then smiled up at Elijah. "Congratulations on baby number three. I can't believe Jazz and Ana are due the same month." It seemed the more she wanted children, the more people in her friendship circle were having them. The little pang that was becoming familiar tweaked her heart.

"Rose is putting in for a sister this time." A special light in his Spanish-moss-colored eyes shone brightly as he spoke of his eldest daughter. He nodded to the man sitting across from her. "Enjoy your dinner. Choice of dessert is on me. I recommend the strawberry cheesecake cobbler."

Adjusting her napkin on her lap, Resa smiled at Steve, her latest attempt to finding the other half of the dream she harbored in her heart.

Steve did not return her smile. He was frowning at the retreating restaurant owner. So he wasn't overly charming. That was okay. Darren had been full of charm, and it had only distracted her.

"What's wrong?" She tried to think what might have offended him.

"He was flirting with you while I was sitting right here. Then he offered to pay for your dessert." He leaned over the table. "A man does not offer a gift to another man's date. You should have turned him down."

Not sure she'd heard right, Resa blinked and gave herself time to process his words. "It was for both of us. I'm their midwife. We've known each other forever. He didn't mean anything by it other than as a nice gesture." One of the reasons Emma thought she might get along well with Steve was that he had also been strung along in his last relationship. He'd been engaged when he'd found out she was seeing someone else. Did he have baggage Resa didn't want to unpack?

"It must be nice to be part of a small community. I would think it would be a lovely place to spend summers." Picking up his fork, he pulled off a piece of his snapper.

Okay, so maybe she'd read too much into his earlier comment. "It is. The population triples. My favorite time on the beach is fall. This is a great place to raise kids all year long. How are you liking Port Del Mar?"

"It was a bit too quiet for me at first. But now that summer is here, I'm enjoying it. It would be the perfect place for a summer house. I've started looking for work in Austin. I miss the city. But having a vacation house here would be the best of both worlds."

"Oh." She hadn't expected that. After eating a piece of her fried shrimp, she dug into the best mac and cheese she had ever eaten. Closing her eyes, she enjoyed the creamy richness.

"You know the enriched flour and cheese in that dish is counteractive to good health. If you are wanting to start a family soon, you might want to think about what you put into your body." He eyed the empty breadbasket. "I've never had a date eat all the bread before." He took a bite of his summer vegetable medley.

Had she eaten all of the biscuits? *Wait.* Was he body shaming her?

He waved a fork at her. "Those extra pounds can make it difficult to conceive. And at your age, you want to be at peak physical condition."

She stared at him. "You know I'm a midwife, right?"

He went on as if she hadn't spoken. "Emma told me how important it is to you to marry and have children. It's refreshing to just be upfront about it at our age. We don't have time to play games. Time we don't have. As we get older, the food we eat affects us more, especially women."

Dinner forgotten; her fork hit the plate. She

blinked, unable to process the words coming out of his mouth.

He must have taken her silence as encouragement to continue.

"I mean if it's an every-once-in-a-while treat, no harm, right?" He grinned and winked at her as if he was being charming.

*Oh no.* How could she politely get out of this without jeopardizing her relationship with Emma at work?

He was going on about something else now. She had not made an exit plan and, with no car, she was trapped. Where was Elijah?

"Tia Resa!"

Still shell-shocked, she turned to the sound of her name without really paying attention. A small body slammed into hers, arms tight around her neck. "I've missed you!"

Laughing, she hugged Lorenzo back. "You saw me this morning at breakfast."

"But that was so long ago. The sun has gone to sleep since then, and I've done so much. I left the door unlatched. The chickens were attacked, and we had to go to the back pasture—"

"Lorenzo." The sharp, cool voice of his uncle cut him off. "Resa is at dinner with a guest. You can't interrupt."

"Oh, he is always welcome to say hi and

give me a hug." She hugged the five-year-old again, and he giggled.

Steve stood, folding his napkin and laying it on the table. "Hello. I'm Steven Harper." He held out his hand to Enzo. "You must be Teresa's oldest brother. I can see the family resemblance. It's a true pleasure to meet you." The men shook hands, but before either Resa or Enzo could correct him, he kept talking. "I'm a great judge of character and can read people very well. It's a gift. I have a feeling we will be seeing a great deal of each other." He winked at her.

Resa couldn't believe the words coming out of this man's mouth.

And he kept talking.

She glanced at Enzo. He was holding a to-go bag. There was no reading his expression. *Family resemblance?* They were both tall, but that was it. The only thing they had in common was dark-brown hair and the nationality their ancestors shared. This date had to come to an end.

She tried to give Enzo the help-me-I'm-trapped look, but his cold gaze stayed on her date as if trying to solve a puzzle.

"Hi!" The energetic five-year-old broke into the man's monologue. "I'm Lorenzo Gruene Flores Hernandez. I'm five. We came to get dinner because my *tío*—" Enzo put a hand on the boy's shoulder.

"Sorry, there's been…" He finally glanced at Resa but after one blink, he was back to Steve. Her shoulders fell.

"Uh, I was saying… Sorry to interrupt, but there has been a family emergency." He turned back to her. "Dolly and Reba have gotten into some trouble, and I need your medical assistance on the ranch."

Dolly and Reba? Those were two of Ana's hens. All of her chickens had been named after her favorite musicians. "Oh. Of course." She shot out of her chair.

He had received her message and was getting her out of there. She grabbed her bag. "I'm sorry, Steve. It was nice meeting you." She paused. "But I really like carbs, so I don't think this will work out." Opening her wallet, she removed a twenty and laid it on the table. Enzo gently took her arm and led her out.

Once outside, she breathed. "Thank you."

"You apologized to that man." His tone was a little accusatory.

"It wasn't his fault it didn't work out, and he seemed to think it was going along perfectly, according to what he told *my brother.*"

Enzo shook his head. "We look nothing alike."

"To be fair, we do have the same hair color. A lot of people just see coloring and not features."

"You have hints of red in your hair that reflect light." He didn't even glance her way. "I do not. Mine's just dark."

If she didn't know him, she'd be flattered at the detailed description. "You do see intricacies no one else does. I'm sure it makes you good at your job." A job that was far away from here.

She stopped at the edge of the sidewalk. "Could you give me a ride home? Steve insisted on picking me up and driving to our date."

Lorenzo took her hand into his small one as they crossed the parking lot.

Enzo guided them down the sidewalk to his sister's silver SUV. "Steve seemed sure you would be seeing him again." He cut her a side glance. "He's a good judge of character. He said so himself."

His delivery was dry, so she missed the mockery at first. Then she chuckled. "Oh, sarcasm. I like it."

"Ana's Yukon is over here. I'll drop you off at your house. It's not too far out of the way."

She did a double take. He'd made another joke. Going to the passenger side, she tried to open the door but, of course, it was locked. Smiling, she waited until she heard a beep.

With a defeated sigh, she slid in and pulled her seat belt across her. This night ended up a bust. She didn't want to even think about all the questions everyone was going to ask. What was Steve going to tell his sister-in-law? She would see Emma on Monday morning.

Enzo stood next to the opened back door. Was he waiting for Lorenzo? Where was he?

"Come on, buddy. Get in your booster so we can get dinner home to your mom while it's still warm."

"I want to go to the store and get flowers for Momma. She likes flowers. The real kind, not fake."

"No. We're going straight home while the food is still warm. We also need to check on the chickens. Your mother needs to know what happened."

"I don't want to do what you say."

Resa twisted around. *What is going on with Lorenzo?* He had his arms crossed and the scowl that warned of a temper looked about to explode.

"I'm too big for the car seat. I want to take flowers to Momma. I want my daddy!"

Enzo took a step back and rubbed his neck. He looked utterly lost. "Lorenzo. Get in the car. Your dad's not here, and your mom needs dinner."

"You're a liar. You told that man—"

"Lorenzo. Get in the car." Enzo's voice was calm and steady as he reached for his nephew.

"No." The little boy twisted away from his uncle and started crying. "I want Daddy."

Taking her seat belt off, Resa got out and went to Lorenzo. People were walking through the parking lot and giving them sideways glances. "Sweetheart, your mom is waiting for you. I know you're upset but throwing a fit in the parking lot is not going to help. Let's go home."

"Are you coming?" He threw his tiny arms around her neck. "Dogs got in the chicken pen. I didn't close the gate all the way. Momma is going to be mad, and I'm not supposed to make her upset. Daddy told me it's bad for her and the baby."

"Oh, sweetheart."

His sob rattled the little chest pressed against her. "Please come." He begged. "Momma will be happy if you can save Dolly and Reba, and Tío Enzo doesn't know anything about chickens. He was looking stuff up on his phone."

"It's going to be okay. Let's get you in your seat." After helping Lorenzo up, she glanced over at his uncle.

The look of uncertainty tweaked at her heart. Enzo stuffed his hands in his pockets. "You should join us. I'm sure you know more about chickens and Lorenzo than I do. And you didn't get to finish your dinner, so I owe you. Will you come?"

"Yes." She kissed Lorenzo on the cheek. "I'll come over."

With everyone in the SUV, Enzo headed down the long strip of road to the ranch. Ana loved those hens. "Where are Reba and Dolly now?" She asked.

"They're on the screened-in porch wrapped in blankets. I read that chickens in shock need to be kept warm and isolated from the other hens, so we placed them in two dog crates that were in the red barn. One has an injured wing, but the other is unmarked."

He glanced in the rearview mirror. "Lorenzo was a champ. He helped a lot. Once, your mom accidentally left a latch undone on the bull's pen. It was a mess, but we helped get the cows all back, just like you helped me take care of the hens. She'll understand."

Enzo glanced at her and then back to the road. The wind pushed hard against the side of the SUV.

Silence filled the inside of the vehicle. No music or chatting, just nature throwing its weight around outside. "I think there's a storm coming in."

With a nod, she replied. "Forecast says it'll rain soon."

Great. They'd been reduced to talking about the weather. She looked out the window. The sky was thick with clouds, and the moon and stars were hidden tonight.

Enzo lowered his voice and leaned to the side, closer to her. "It's not going well. I don't know what I did. It's like he's mad at me."

She twisted to check on Lorenzo. His head was against the window and his mouth hung open in deep sleep. "He crashed. Did he have a nap today?"

"He threw a fit and said he didn't need one. I wasn't sure if he still had them at his age. It was easier to go along with him. I hate to admit it, but I have no clue what to do. I thought bonding with him would be much easier. It's been a tough day for us both. That is the third time he's said I've lied about something."

"He's always been very sensitive and gets overstimulated easily. He also has a very literal mind and things are black and white for him. He didn't understand the story about the family emergency and my medical help. It probably confused him with his mother's bedrest."

"I didn't even think of that. But I didn't lie.

Ana thinks of those chickens as family. She thinks of you as family too. So this is a family emergency." His voice was low, but the edge was back, as if his honor had been challenged.

"No, you didn't lie. Have you told Ana about the dogs? Did they have tags? We need to make sure they're off the ranch."

"They took off as soon as they saw us. I didn't see collars. My sister loves those chickens, and I don't want to needlessly upset her. I want to make sure the hens are okay before telling her anything. Would you mind coming out and looking at them? If we have to give her bad news, I think it'd be better coming from you."

"You're just being a chicken. Ha. Ha. See what I did there?"

He groaned. "So how did you end up living on the ranch?"

"When I moved back to town over a year ago, I moved in with my mom, but I knew I needed my own place. Quickly. Your sister offered me one of the old homesteads to rent. It's small, but it's perfect for me."

"Ana asked what I thought about renting the house out yearly instead of a weekend rental. One was more money, and one was less hassle. I supported her either way. She told me she was going with the one that was easier for her to manage. She didn't tell me you were the renter, though."

"Would you have said no?"

He shook his head. "It's just strange she didn't tell me."

She eyed his to-go bags. "You don't happen to have mac and cheese in those, do you?"

He grinned and then winked before turning the SUV into the drive up to the ranch. "Who would go to the Painted Dolphin and not get the mac and cheese?"

That unexpected grin created a fluttering in her chest. *No. None of that.*

She leaned back and closed her eyes. Enzo was turning out to be just her type. But dating guys like him had left her thirty and nowhere close to having the family she dreamed of. Her sister, Josie, had told her that if tonight's date didn't work out, she already had another lined up with a man who lived over the bridge, close enough. Josefina had gone on and on about how perfect the man was for her.

But the thought of another date exhausted her. Resa hated the whole process. Why couldn't she just find a guy who wanted to hang out with her? Getting to know people was not as fun as it sounded. It would have been so much easier if Steve Harper had been the one. She should know better than to expect easy.

If she wanted a chance at reaching her goal, she needed to stick to the plan the women in her life had set up. Leaning back against the leather headrest, she glanced at Enzo.

Should she put her husband search on hold while Enzo was in town? He was here to help his sister, but it wasn't going well. He might just cause more stress for Ana and Lorenzo. He had saved her tonight, so maybe she could return the favor. He was going to need a lot of help with the ranch and his nephew. Yes. Helping him would help Ana. It had nothing to do with those smothering good looks or lost soulful eyes.

He was leaving soon. She'd get back to her plan then.

# Chapter Four

After putting the dinner in the kitchen, Enzo went back to the porch. The red hen named Reba sat on Lorenzo's lap. Resa was gently checking her wing. With a nod from her, his nephew placed the hen back in the crate they had made comfortable for her. She went to the water and drank.

"That's a good sign, right?" he asked.

They both turned in surprise, shocked to see him standing behind them. Resa closed her eyes and placed her hand over her heart. "You have to stop sneaking up on me like that."

Leaning on a post, he crossed his arms and smiled. "Maybe you need better survival skills. I wasn't quiet." He came over and peered into the crate.

Resa stood. "My survival skills are just fine, and so are the girls. It's safe to give Ana a good report."

His small nephew was sitting next to the other hen, gently stroking her feathers down her neck. "Dolly is eating and drinking too. I'm going to tell Momma what happened."

He wanted to take the boy in his arms and reassure him, but he doubted Lorenzo would let him. Enzo settled for putting his hand on the boy's small shoulder. "She'll understand, and she'll be proud of how hard you worked to make them better."

No response.

Giving up, he went to the door and opened it. "It's time to fix the plates for dinner. Lorenzo, get your mom."

"Yes, sir." His nephew slipped past him and ran through the kitchen to the hallway.

Resa followed Lorenzo inside the house. What was he doing wrong with the five-year-old? After one last check on the chickens, he went to the kitchen, where Resa was pulling glasses from the cabinet.

"How do I get him to trust me?" She had to have some insight he could use. "He doesn't call me *tío* or uncle most of the time. But he calls you *tía* and you're not his aunt."

"Ana and I spend a lot of time together. Right now, he's uncertain about everything and doesn't really know you. Give him time." She took plates out of the cabinet.

Time. Something he might not have enough of. As soon as his parents returned, he would be going back to Denver. He put ice in the glasses and then got the fresh pitcher of sweet tea from the refrigerator. "Is it okay for Ana to make tea?"

She smiled. "Yes. It's good for her to move a bit."

They worked around each other until the table was set.

Hands on her hips, Resa looked at him. "How long *do* you plan on staying?"

"I'm not sure. Dad and Mom are working on getting someone to cover for them so they can come home early. As soon as they're here, my attendance will no longer be required."

"That's not true."

Ana followed Lorenzo into the room and put her arm through Enzo's. His nephew ran to Resa. Of course, he did.

"You're just trying to sneak away." Ana squeezed him closer as if to hold him to the ranch. "Fall is right around the corner. It's my favorite time on the ranch. You haven't been home since we started doing the Fall Festival. We're hosting it for the first time this year. There is even a pumpkin patch in the east pasture behind PaPa Jack's and Mama Boo's house."

"You're a pumpkin farmer now?" He pulled out the chair for her. She never ceased to amaze him. "I don't think we should be doing any hosting this year."

"It's fine. I can handle paperwork and planning. We can hire extra help for the physical labor. The Wilsons' pecan trees are showing off this year. The Mullers have figs and other fall vegetables. Do you remember Juan Martinez and Julie Meyer? They are growing apples and have enough to make cider and preserves. There's a new flower farm and—"

He held up his hands. "I'm exhausted just listening to this. You're in charge? And who grows apples on the coast of Texas? Isn't it too warm?"

She shrugged. "We've tried to warn them, but they're determined. I have a lengthy list of local farmers who are using that weekend to move a lot of product to get people to travel to the beach for the fall. We want to get the word out, so there will be plenty for everyone to do, including you. Don't rush back to Denver as soon as the parents arrive."

He glanced at Resa for help. There was no way his sister should be worrying about some Fall Festival. She ignored him and helped Lorenzo fill his plate.

"And you, Resa. I'm so glad you're here.

I haven't heard a word about your date. Did Enzo drag you away from Mr. Perfect because he didn't know what to do with the chickens?"

"No. Let's just say it was a bust. Enzo and your son actually rescued me, along with saving the chickens tonight."

"Oh no. We had high hopes for him." She didn't sound particularly sorry. "I'm delighted my big brother was there to save the day."

"I didn't do any saving. She had it under control. I just gave her a ride home."

"Sit down and relax, Enzo. I think that scowl is permanent. Mom always warned you it would get stuck that way if you didn't take it easy. You're too serious." She tossed a cheddar biscuit at him.

He caught it and took a bite. He did miss his sister. No one else ever challenged his mood. Except for Resa, but she didn't count. He couldn't let her count. His gut told him that would be dangerous. The biscuit was gone in two bites. "Someone has to be."

Lorenzo's eyes were wide as he stared at his mother. "Momma, did you throw food at someone?"

"Just your uncle." She laughed. "He deserved it."

"But we should never throw food. That's a time-out."

The poor kid looked so confused by his mother's behavior. Lorenzo would probably blame Enzo.

Resa nodded with overly dramatized seriousness. "Usually, yes. It's poor manners. But once your baby sister is old enough to follow you around and talk your ears off, you'll discover good behavior goes out the window. Siblings will bring out the worst and best in you."

"I would lean heavily on the worst." Enzo winked at his nephew.

This time, a smaller chunk of biscuit bounced off his cheek. "Your mom's aim is better than it used to be." Plucking the piece off the table, he tossed it in his mouth. With a lightness in his chest, he grinned and dug into his mac and cheese.

Both women laughed, adding to poor Lorenzo's confusion. There was light chitchat as the women talked about the day. Lorenzo filled his mom in about the other chickens and how many eggs he'd gathered before the dog drama.

His meal finished, Enzo went to the freezer and pulled out the Blue Bell ice cream. He offered to make crumbled cookie shakes in their grandmother's old mint-green Hamilton, and everyone said yes. Even his nephew smiled at him.

After the shakes were gone, Lorenzo jerked his head up and blinked.

"Oh, sweetheart, let me take you to bed." Ana pushed back the hair that had fallen over his eyes. "You need a haircut."

"No! Daddy takes me to cut my hair." He crossed his arms and scowled.

Ana shook her head but gave him a gentle smile. "When you do that, you look just like your *tío*."

Enzo and his nephew stared at each other for a moment, and Resa laughed. "He really does."

"No. I look like my daddy."

Giving his nephew a gentle nudge, he rolled his eyes. "My sister and her *amiga* are *loco* in the *cabeza*. Why don't we leave them to finish their talk of the Fall Festival and you can show me your room? Do you have a story I can read? I like to read before I go to bed."

The suspicion was back on the little guy's face.

"That's a great idea." Ana said. "That would be a great help. Thank you, Enzo. Come here and give me a kiss good night, little man."

Slipping off his chair as if he'd received a life sentence, Lorenzo went to his mom and hugged her. "Momma, you need to go to bed too. I heard Daddy say you need to rest."

"I am. Your *tía* Resa will make sure I do.

We just need to finish up a few things she is doing for me, okay?"

He nodded and then slipped his fingers between Enzo's.

Holding still for a moment, Enzo studied the difference in the size of their hands. The contact had startled him. His nephew was so small and fragile. It would be easy for someone to break him. Enzo shook his head. This was why he had to get back to work. There were bad people in the world who needed to be stopped. It was his job to protect the weak. He had no clue what he was doing on the ranch.

Instead of reading, Enzo ended up answering questions about Lorenzo's dad. His nephew wanted to know how they'd met, if they were friends, and anything else Enzo knew about his father. It took longer than he had anticipated. His nephew had a gift for asking questions, and Enzo had no clue how to wrap it up without upsetting the boy.

Unable to keep his eyes open any longer, Lorenzo nodded off to sleep, and Enzo used all his training to back out of the room without stirring the sleepy five-year-old. He paused at the door. His lungs stopped as emotions he didn't recognize paralyzed him.

Ana was four years younger than he, so he had clear memories of her at this age. Where did the time slip away to? How was it possible he was now sneaking out of her child's room instead of hers? Some days, he just felt so old.

Where were his choices in this life taking him?

Forcing air in through his nose, he shut the door. As he made his way downstairs, he stopped at each framed photo.

It was a collection of his family history. His great-grandparents stood with two horses, each holding a lead. His great-grandmother was in a full dress with all of the layers. How had she managed to ranch in that outfit in the Texas heat? His grandfather was a curly headed toddler sitting on the back of the ranch's prized stallion. True Arrow's bloodline was still the foundation of the ranch's herd. Family pride in the reputation of their cattle horses was well founded.

At the base of the stairs was a picture of Ana and Enzo riding on Black Arrow. He'd held three-year-old Ana close. He hadn't wanted her to get hurt on the big horse. He had been the first boy in several generations, and they'd all assumed he would take over the ranch.

The last picture was of Lorenzo on a blood bay held by Ana. Julian was in the picture too, posing in front of a blue roan Enzo had never seen before. In front of the smiling young family was a healthy collection of trophies and championship ribbons.

They were all connected. Each generation was building on the last. Where did he fit into all of this?

He had never really thought about leaving a legacy. When he was gone, he would just fade away. The agency would replace him. He was just a gear in their machine. They had probably already replaced him.

All the reflection he had been doing since crossing the threshold of this old home made him uncomfortable. His muscles tense, he filled his lungs and relaxed his clenched fist. The FBI gave him purpose. He had a good life.

He'd call his parents tomorrow and put the pressure on them to come home. They would be much more useful to Ana at this time than he was.

He stood in front of the door to the old library, which had served as an office for as long as he could remember and knocked. It was his sister's bedroom now. The whole house belonged to her. Before leaving for Peru, their parents had moved into a travel trailer and handed the running of the ranch over to Ana.

No one had even asked if he was interested. But then again, he had made it clear even as a young child that he'd wanted to leave. His sister would be the fourth generation of women to run the ranch. Their grandmother had been the only child of Captain Gruene, one of the founding families of Port Del Mar.

He knocked again, a little louder this time. Were they ignoring him? Maybe the women didn't want him to join them. Taking a step back, he debated whether to knock again or go to his room.

"Come in," came a frustrated reply.

Okay. In he went. He eased the door open. The office had always been his sister's favorite place after the barns. As a kid, she'd spent hours hiding under the ornate wood desk, reading and drawing.

Large windows allowed the soft glow of the full moon to coat the room in a light gold. There was a bed where the desk used to be. Ana sat in the center, nested in blankets and surrounded by papers and books.

He didn't like the frown on her face as she squinted at the laptop. She shifted and wrote notes in a journal. His tough, larger-than-life sister looked fragile. He wasn't used to this. She was usually a ball of energy, just like her son. Being still didn't suit her.

"Mom and Julian told me your doctor said no stress. That looks like a lot of stress."

With a sigh, she leaned back on the pillows.

"You and my doctor—" she cut a glare at Resa, who was sitting next to the bed in one of the surprisingly super feminine chairs from his grandmother's days "—should go discuss it over a cup of coffee I'm not allowed to have and leave me in peace."

A scowl wrinkled his forehead before he could school his expression. "Resa's your doctor?" He thought she was a nurse.

"She's my midwife. She's also a PA. We are making decisions together."

"But you also have a real doctor, right?" The temp in the room dropped to subzero. What was wrong with him? Every word he spoke was usually thought out and intentional.

Resa stiffened. Hands folded, she pressed her knuckles against her full lips.

"Sorry. I didn't mean it like that. But this has become a high-risk pregnancy, right? You would need a specialist."

Resa took a very visible breath and then relaxed her shoulders. "It's a high-risk pregnancy, but not delivery. We are monitoring her and the baby. Our goal is to get her to thirty-six weeks so she can deliver at home. If she goes into labor before that, she will go to the hospital. The clinic I work with has an OBGYN and a pediatrician. She has seen both."

He carefully went to the foot of her bed.

"Sorry. I have no experience in this world, so I might ask stupid questions." His sister smiled at him, letting him know all was forgiven. Resa, not so much. He grinned. That poor Steve guy hadn't had a chance.

Resa, arms crossed, turned her glare from him to his sister and took a deep breath. "But he is right. Stress in any form is not good for you." She waved at the documents littering the bed.

"I know, but this is for the festival." She handed him a piece of paper with a list of names. "These are the vendors." A yellow folder came his way. "These are the repairs and updates that need to be made in the arena and pole barn. There's a meeting with all the stakeholders next Tuesday. If you don't feel comfortable going alone, I can go with you."

"No." Resa said the single word right along with him.

Ana rolled her eyes. "Here." This time, a purple binder was handed off. "All the information you need to know about the other ranches and farms that are taking part is in this binder. There are a total of twenty-three this year. It's almost double anything we've had before. A few people think we've grown too big too fast, but I know we can do this and make it productive and profitable for everyone involved. Don't embarrass me or prove me wrong. Failure is not an option."

"Never is." He scanned the cover sheet of names and addresses. Some he recognized as long-time families and farms from Port Del Mar, but there were more he didn't know. "Maybe we should bring the number down. With your health—"

"Don't even go there. If you can't do it, I will."

"No. No. I got it. Don't give it another thought." He tucked the loose papers in the three-inch binder and snapped it shut. "I've got this." He didn't, but he would have it under control before Tuesday.

Resa reached over and took Ana's hand. "You don't have to threaten your brother. There are people who want to help. I'm right here." She looked up at Enzo and held his gaze. "I can go with you." Her phone chimed with a notification. Glancing down, she frowned.

"Is it Darren again?" His sister turned to him. "Her ex has been calling her all day. That's harassment, right?"

Resa looked at her phone. "He just sent a text. It's about Princess Leia." Standing, she crossed the room while reading the text. "He says it's an emergency. It might just be a way to get me on the phone, but I have to take it just in case something *is* wrong with her." She closed the door behind her.

"Princess Leia?" he asked.

"The cat they adopted together. When she came home, she let him keep her because she thought the move would be too much for the cat and create unnecessary stress. As a kitten, she'd suffered major trauma. Between you and me, Resa felt guilty breaking up with him and thought he needed the cat more than she did for emotional support." She moved some books to the nightstand. "Her heart and sense of loyalty kept her in the relationship way past the point when she should have walked. Her coming home was a good move. He wasn't going to change."

"Did he hurt her?" A cold rage burned his blood.

"Oh, nothing like that. They just wanted different things in life, hugely different things, and he strung her along making promises he never kept. She couldn't compromise her dreams any longer." His sister frowned at the door. "I hope he's not messing with her."

She leaned forward as much as her belly allowed. "I have a really bad feeling about this call. If he convinces her to go pick up Leia, she can't do it alone. I don't know what game he's playing, but you need to go. I would but—" With a grimace, she sat back.

"Ana?" He stepped forward, concerned.

When Resa entered the room, his relief was immediate. "Something's wrong. She's in pain."

"No. No." Ana waved them off. "It was just a foot in the kidney."

"Are you sure?" Resa asked, laying a hand on Ana's belly.

She nodded. "I promise. I'm not going to do anything to risk my baby girl. That includes the Fall Festival. Enzo has agreed to take the lead if you help him."

He narrowed his eyes at Ana. He had forgotten how clever his little sister was at getting people to do what she wanted. Resa looked at him, and he nodded. What else was there to do?

"So what did the sloth want? Is Princess Leia okay?"

Resa looked down. "Yeah. Um. His wife will be giving birth in the next couple of months, and she is threatening to take Princess Leia to the shelter. She says cats suffocate babies."

"What?" Ana sat up, her eyes wide. "Did you say 'wife'? He's married and is having a *baby*?"

"Seems so." Resa's voice sounded as if it crawled through glass to be heard. She cleared her throat. "If I don't come pick her up in the next few days, Kimberly, that's his wife, is dumping her at a shelter. He didn't want that to happen, so he's been trying to get a hold of me to see if I'm willing to save *our* cat. That's what he called her."

*Was she about to cry?*

Ana reached out and took Resa's hand. "I know you're over him, but this still has to hurt. He told you over and over he was not ready for the whole kids-and-marriage thing and now this? Men. They're idiots."

His sister turned on him and glared like it was all his fault. He knew there was no way to soundly argue the statement, so he remained silent.

"I'll be okay." Resa closed her eyes for a moment and then smiled as if she had just righted her world. "I miss my kitty cat, so this is good news. I'll get her back. She can be the start of my cat-lady phase. I told him I can be in San Antonio Saturday."

"Oh, that's perfect. Enzo can go with you." Turning, Ana looked straight at him. "Remember Jessica Radcliffe?" She gave him the I'm-your-little-sister-and-you-love-me look, so he braced himself for something he wouldn't like and nodded.

"She lives in Seguin now. Last week, I was supposed to pick up some of Lorenzo's baby furniture that Jessica borrowed, but—" she waved at herself "—since it's on the way to San Antonio, you can make a full day out of it. Jessica's also going to cut Lorenzo's hair. Since his dad can't be here, it'll help that you're with him."

Enzo hoped that was true, but serious doubts twisted his stomach. He was no replacement for Julian.

Resa crossed her arms. "I'm a big girl. I can get the cat on my own. I don't need bodyguards. And it's a much longer trip than just going to Seguin."

Ana yawned. "I'm ready to call it a night." Laying her head on the pillow, she reached her hand out to her best friend. "Don't face the sloth and his bride alone, please. I'll worry all day." She used the one argument she knew Resa would give in to.

"You're strong enough and more than capable of picking the cat up, but why do it alone if you don't have to, right, Enzo?"

Sighing with resignation, he nodded. "It will be more efficient if we get this done all in one day. And backup is always a good option. I'm sure it will make the trip easier for Lorenzo if you're there." And that was the truth. He wasn't sure he could get his nephew in the car let alone agree to a haircut.

"Okay. A road trip on Saturday it is." Resa didn't sound that thrilled as she gathered the papers and books. "Enzo and I will handle the Tuesday meeting. Just email us any questions you want to ask or information you have."

Ana reached for her laptop. Enzo closed it and sat it on her nightstand. "Tomorrow." He leaned over and kissed her forehead. "They say I'm stubborn. 'Night, sis."

"Good night."

He and Resa walked down the hall in silence. Entering the kitchen, Resa turned to him, the papers and books clasped tightly to her torso. "I'll take this and go through them. Organize the information we need. Once I do that, we can make a plan of action."

"You know going through data, organizing it, and making a plan is one of the things I do for a living, right?"

Setting the collection on the table, she laughed. "It's all yours then."

He grinned. "That was too easy. I don't remember you being this agreeable as a kid."

She shrugged. "Listen, you don't have to go with me to pick up my cat. It will add almost two hours to your day. I can manage facing my ex alone."

He leaned a hip on the counter and studied her for a minute. She had to be hurting. He could see it in her eyes. Some of that light he admired had gone out. Her joy and love of life was usually so bright, but it was dimmed now.

He did *not* like this guy. "But I'm not sure I would survive facing my sister when she discovered I let you handle the retrieval without backup."

"Oh, the big bad special agent is afraid of his little sister. And you make the *retrieval* sound much more exciting than picking up a cat from an ex-boyfriend."

"There can be a great deal of psychological landmines in a meeting like that. Me being there gives you an excuse to get the cat and leave. We can be in and out in less than five minutes."

"Okay. Deal. I'll block off the whole day so we can leave at sunrise, if needed. Let me know the order of events so I can tell Darren what time to expect us."

"You're not going to let me plan a sneak attack?" The guy deserved to be taken down a peg or two. Resa was the most giving person he knew. Her heart was always too big, even back in school. It had gotten her and his sister in trouble more than once. This Darren guy had obviously hurt her, and Enzo wanted to return the favor.

He wasn't sure where this need to do some damage to this guy was coming from. Being detached from emotions was part of his job. Maybe being home was putting him in a different mindset.

Resa's laughter warmed the room. "I'm tempted to let you, but that would be petty, and my momma taught me to be the better person."

And she was. She always had been. Even when he'd needled and poked at her, she'd glared and growled a little, but he'd always been able to count on her turning up with a smile in a matter of minutes. Resa's range of emotions made him think of rainbows and God's promise of hope.

He needed that in his life right now. A reminder that darkness would always be smothered by light. Even though he hadn't realized it until now, he'd needed to come home.

But the visit was temporary. He was needed on the frontlines to stop the darkness from invading.

This short break would recharge him so he could go back to his job. He was needed there. His sister had the ranch and would be back on her feet soon.

Resa wanted someone to build a family and plant roots with. She deserved to live her dreams, and his job was to protect people like her. They were the reason he faced down the darkness. He did it so the light could shine.

The warmth he found in her eyes needed to be protected and cherished. He was leaving. His skills weren't required here, but they were essential to the FBI.

He was not a family man. After so many years on the job, darkness had crept into every corner of his brain. To the point where he saw threats and danger everywhere.

Just the other night, he'd nearly hurt Resa while she'd been setting up a surprise for his sister. That darkness made it impossible for him to bring children into this world. There was a reason divorce rates were so high in the Bureau.

If he didn't get remarried, he wouldn't add to the statistics. Not that he was thinking of marriage. He snorted. Not even in the deepest parts of his mind would he ever consider marriage again. His job was to protect people like his sister and Resa. Not just her, the whole Espinoza family. They were good. He would face down the malice for them.

They deserved to sleep at night without worry. Resa should have the husband of her dreams. He had too many nightmares to even think about that position ever being his.

# Chapter Five

Resa went through her bag to make sure she had everything she might need. She'd never understood the use of a small purse. But then again, she'd been raised by a woman who'd been prepared to handle anything when it came to her seven children.

She fingered the colorful frayed tassel tied to the zipper. Why had she agreed to this trip? She should have just gone to get the cat. Sitting in the car for two hours with Enzo Flores was not her idea of fun. At least they would have Lorenzo with them. She loved that kid.

A loud knock on the door startled her. Enzo was here. She scanned the room to make sure it was straight.

One. Two. Three. Each knock was full of confidence. Why was she hesitating to open the door? It was just Enzo. All through school, he had annoyed her. He'd never treated her badly. He'd just done what he'd thought he needed to do to protect his sister...from her. The only reason he'd agreed to go along with this trip was for Ana.

She took a deep breath in and slowly pushed the air out of her lungs until there was nothing left. Stepping forward, she opened the door and faced Enzo's fist, ready to knock against the wood again. With a gasp, she leaned back, the low heel of her summer sandals catching on the edge of the frayed rug.

Strong hands caught her and saved her from falling. "Whoa, there." Enzo steadied her and then stepped back. He looked so sharp in a starched, white, buttoned shirt with a dark gray jacket. It looked as if he was going to work. That was because he thought of her as a job, just one more duty he had to perform. Did he ever relax? Why did that make her sad?

"Sorry about that. I'm trying to take you out at every turn. Are you okay? I was getting worried." He glanced at his watch.

She didn't know anyone who still wore an old-fashion wristwatch.

He looked back up. His intense stare seared right through her. *Breathe in. Breathe out.*

"We agreed to leave at six thirty, correct? Am I too early?"

"Yes. I mean no. You're not early. Yes, we agreed to six thirty. Um, it's six fifteen. But it's all good." Why did she sound breathless? "I was double-checking my bag. A good Espinoza is prepared for everything."

He grinned and raised one brow. "What does a bad Espinoza do?"

With a twist of her lips, she pretended to give it deep thought. "They would have to face the wrath of my mother. I don't think that has ever happened. So I have no answer to your question." She gripped the worn leather strap of her favorite bag.

With a nod, he stepped back, allowing her room to move past him and onto the small porch. Parked next to her little black Ford Focus was a lifted Ford Bronco from the seventies. Really? They both drove Fords...from way different decades. The top and bottom of his vintage vehicle was the color of golden sand. Running along the center were strips of a faded sunset. Not the car she would have ever expected practical Enzo to drive.

"This is yours?"

"Yes, ma'am. I can't tell if you're shocked in a good way or horrified." He went to the passenger side and opened the door. "It was my grandfather's. My dad's dad. It was the first car he bought for himself. Custom ordered it in

1968. When I was a teen, I helped him rebuild the engine. When I graduated from A&M, he gave it to me. I was the first in his family to attend college."

He held his hand out and helped her step up into the seat. The breeze played with the edges of her delicate skirt. Several gauzy layers flared from the fitted waist. Now, she was doubting her choice of her super feminine summer dress.

As soon as she'd seen it in Bianca's Boutique, she'd loved the bold prints of yellow and orange flowers on such a soft fabric. But the impractical fairy-tale dress was not made for climbing in and out of a vehicle three feet off the ground. What had made her want to wear it today?

"Well, at least I won't lose you," he said as she adjusted the gauzy material. "Nice color."

"It actually coordinates with the sunset on the side of your monster truck."

He frowned and shifted back to look at the side of his SUV. Then his brows shot up and he grinned as his gaze moved back to her. "Um. You're right. It's like a muted sunset. I never thought of it like that." With a double tap on the side of the Bronco, he closed her door and walked around to the driver's side.

Seat belt on, she held her bag in her lap and

turned to greet a grumpy-looking Lorenzo. "Good morning. Are you ready to get your hair cut?"

"No. I'm waiting for my dad to come home."

Enzo was snapping his seat belt in place. "Your mom wants to see your eyes. And for you to look good when he does come home."

Crossing his arms, Lorenzo pouted. "Someone should stay with Mom today. I don't want to go."

With a sigh, Enzo turned the key. The engine was the only sound as they pulled on to the two-lane country road. It didn't take Lorenzo long to fall asleep. "You do look nice," he said without taking his focus off the road.

"Did you just compliment me?" She turned with narrowed eyes. *"¿Que pasa?"*

He grinned as he gave a two-finger greeting to a truck heading east and then gave her another quick glance before focusing on the road again. He had a pair of dark aviators, so she couldn't see his eyes, but she was sure he was mocking her.

He shook his head and sighed as if he were being forced to deal with an unreasonable three-year-old. "Nothing is *up*. I like the dress. That's all. You didn't do this for your ex. Did you?"

"No!" Then she lowered her voice so as not

to disturb Lorenzo. "I would rather not think about Darren." She did want to look her best when meeting his wife. Was that petty?

Opening her purse, she looked for her phone. It wasn't in the side pocket. It was in there somewhere. She hated it when she didn't take the time to put it in the right place.

"Are you okay?" The deep, steady voice stopped her search. How did it feel to always be so certain of your place in this world?

"I'm looking for my phone. It's in here some-where. Ana gave me Jessica's address. It's our first stop." She went back to digging.

"Did you prepare for an apocalypse?"

She really didn't need his sarcasm today. "No. Just for an encounter with an ex who didn't want a family with me and his new preg-nant wife."

He grimaced. "Sorry. It must be tough." His hands at a perfect nine-and-three-o'clock po-sition, he gave her a quick glance. He cleared his throat. "Is there anything I can do to make it go easier? Do you want to talk about it?"

*Oh no.* She didn't even want to think about Darren and his little family, let alone talk about it with Enzo.

"Thank you, it's a kind offer." She found it. "Yay! I have my phone. I'll put Jessica's address in my maps and then I thought we could go over the details for the Fall Festival."

"I already plotted out the route." He gave her another side-eyed glance. "Uh…but if you want to put it in your phone, that works too."

Dropping her hands into her lap, she stared out the windshield. The night sky was still fighting for life in the West. In the side mirror, she could see the promise of a new day and the light brightened the horizon behind them. They were driving in the wrong direction. There was not a piece of her that wanted to face Darren.

Moving forward and making a plan for the future she wanted was not in this direction.

"Do you want to stop and get something to eat?" He interrupted her spiraling thoughts.

Her stomach roiled. The thought of eating didn't sit well, but she didn't want Enzo to know how nervous she was to see Darren. It was embarrassing. She wanted it to be no big deal. "If you're hungry, that's fine. I'm not much of a breakfast person."

"I already ate. I made pancakes for Lorenzo. We brought snacks too. If you need to stop, let me know."

They fell into silence, and Lorenzo's snores filled the cabin. It was early for the little guy. Darren had never been a morning person. He liked living to his own schedule. It was one of the reasons he had put off having a family. Why had he changed his mind?

She wanted to think of something else, anything else. A distraction would be good. That's what she needed. Picking up her phone, she went to her notes. They could go over the festival details.

"I have a question."

She stopped scrolling and glanced up, but Enzo was still staring at the road. She waited.

"About Ana." His voice was low. "I really don't want to offend you, but everything I know tells me she should be under a medical doctor's supervision. Not just any OBGYN, but one that specializes in preterm deliveries. Is it because you're friends that she..." He blew out a puff of air.

"No." Making sure to take a deep breath to ease her spiking blood pressure, Resa opened her notes app. She handled this kind of questioning all the time and it never upset her.

Normally, it was a welcomed opportunity to share her passion with people about the mission she believed God had put in her heart. No reason Enzo should be any different.

Checking to make sure Lorenzo was still sleeping, she started to explain. "Ana didn't have wonderful experiences with traditional hospitals. You know the trouble she had not only conceiving but also taking a pregnancy to term. Amy was her midwife with Lorenzo, and together they were able to get Ana where she wanted to be physically. Amy also recognized the role that anxiety and stress played in Ana's body. When I moved back into the area, Amy was able to finally step back to part-time. She's in her seventies and is still an incredible resource. That's how I became Ana's midwife."

"I didn't know. I understand everything is going fine, but at this point, wouldn't it be safer to be working with a doctor who specializes in high-risk pregnancies?"

She nodded. "We have consulted with a physician. Last month, I drove her to the hospital when she experienced preterm labor."

For the first time, his gaze left the road and darted to her. "Really?"

"I'm not anti-doctor. We work together as a team. Her labor stopped, so they sent her home. I will not do a home birth before thirty-six weeks. Midwifery care has a higher success rate in avoiding PTB."

"PTB. Is that preterm birth? So, if she's too early, they'll go to the hospital."

"Yep. Do you know, by simply walking through the doors of a hospital, a woman increases her chances of a C-section by thirty percent? It can be a lifesaving procedure for mother and baby, but sometimes it's just used because it's the easiest way to avoid a lawsuit."

*Easy, Resa. Breathe.* That last line sounded a little defensive. "I love what I do. God has put this service in my heart. But I'm regulated by the Texas board of nursing, and the medical board, because I have prescriptive authority." *See, I am a professional.* She patted herself on the back.

"Thank you. Not for now. I guess I just remember all the...um...adventures you took my sister on, and it's strange seeing you as an expert in life-and-death situations."

Narrowing her eyes, she tried to figure out what he meant by that. But with those aviators hiding his eyes and his mouth in its usual stiff-upper-lip setting, there was no reading him. "Now that is out of the way, let's organize a list of things we need to do for the festival event."

Her phone had reverted to the screensaver. Ana, Julian and Lorenzo smiled at her from the picture. The little family filled the display with pure joy. It had been taken at the mid-point of Ana's second trimester. One hand on her curving belly.

Her little part of bringing happiness to families should be enough to give her life purpose.

Being unsatisfied made her feel ungrateful for the blessings in her life.

"Resa?" Enzo said her name as if he had called it for the third or fourth time.

"Sorry. I was opening the file."

This time, he looked at her over his glasses, and she could see the concern in the rich brown eyes. With a sigh, he turned his attention back to the road. "When we meet with the ex and his bride, you should stay in the car. I'll retrieve the cat."

For a split second, she loved the idea, but she wasn't a coward. She couldn't and wouldn't allow Darren to make her hide. "No. She's my cat. Darren and, um…" She twisted her lips. She had honestly forgotten the woman's name.

"Kimberly."

"Yeah. I'm not going to cower in your truck. I can take care of my own business." Last thing her self-confidence needed was for Enzo to see her weak. "I got this."

# *Chapter Six*

The sun had cleared the horizon as Enzo pulled into the neat little neighborhood. It was one of the older neighborhoods in the area, established before the average square footage of a house was over two thousand. Lots of the homes here were the size of a dime. Old pecan and giant oak trees lined the sidewalks. A few early risers were jogging or walking the dog, but for the most part, it was quiet.

Brittany had wanted to buy a house in a new subdivision. They hadn't argued, he'd just put her off, claiming to be too busy. Now, he lived alone in a two-bedroom apartment. He wasn't there enough to know his neighbors.

Resa closed her phone and put it away. "Getting a list of the projects completed and a timeline for the ones we need to get done is a great start to the day."

Lorenzo turned away from him and looked to Resa, but he nodded.

"Good. Your mom wants you to cut your hair. So tell me, what would your dad want you to do?"

The bottom lip came out farther than Enzo thought possible. He waited, letting the idea process through the five-year-old's brain. He had already learned that if he let it fall into a power struggle, he would lose. And if he got the boy into the chair for the cut against his will, he would lose any chance of building a real relationship with him. So he waited. He was good at waiting.

After one dramatic sigh, his nephew reached over and unbuckled his seat belt. "Okay. I'll get my hair cut."

Enzo wanted to howl in victory. Getting his way had never felt so good. But he played it cool and helped Lorenzo off the high step of his Bronco. Resa gave him two thumbs-up, her fists held close together where the boy wouldn't see.

The door opened and a petite redhead came out with a toddler on her hip. "Resa." The woman hugged her. "It's been so long. Happy to hear you're back in Port Del Mar." She turned to Enzo with a big smile. The two-year-old hid his face in her neck. "Hi, Enzo.

The efficient way they worked together had surprised him. He was also relieved that she didn't want to talk about her ex or his new wife. That probably made him a bad person, but he had no idea how to deal with those kinds of messy emotions. "I like a good list. Makes any task doable." Was he as boring as he sounded?

She grinned and her brilliant smile lit up his whole Bronco. "I'm learning that they make life so much easier. Having a clear plan and marking stuff off is *so* satisfying. Look at us. Finding common ground."

He held back a snort. "Jessica's house is on the left."

"They know we're coming, right? It's early."

"It's kind of late to be concerned about that." The house, a Craftsman with a deep porch, was next to a French-inspired cottage.

"Maybe we should park and wait until we see movement. I don't want to wake a sleeping mom if her kids are still in bed."

He maneuvered the Bronco so he could pull into the driveway backward. "I called last night to confirm. Scott said he had the furniture in the garage and that Jessica would be ready for Lorenzo. She has a little shop behind the garage. We'll be in and out and on to rescue Princess Leia before lunch." He checked on the small person everyone said looked like him. "Should we wake up Lorenzo?" He was dreading a fight with the boy over the haircut. "What if he says no? I promised Ana I'd seen it done, but I can't tie him to the chair." He turned to Resa. "Can I?"

There was a pretty uptick to the corner of her lips as she shook her head. "No. We'll get it done. Without a rope."

The double-wide door clanked as it rose. A man in his late twenties stood next to a compact SUV. With a smile, he waved for them to move closer. The organized space was a mixture of toys and tools hanging on pegs or stored in labeled containers.

Stepping out of the Bronco, Enzo greeted the man with a handshake.

Jessica's husband, Scott, welcomed them with a bright smile. "Good morning. Thank you for coming early. It's easier to get things done before everyone is awake." He grinned. "You don't really appreciate the little things your parents sacrificed until you have kids."

Enzo nodded, but he didn't have to have kids to know how much his parents had given up for his sister and him. He glanced at Resa. She wanted a family. Was it hard to be around people with kids or to hear stuff like that? He

knew Scott didn't mean anything by it, a was way overanalyzing.

Scott waved to the neatly stacked bab niture behind him. "I think she has a few inside, but this is most of it."

"It looks easy enough to load. The ha is going to be getting Lorenzo to agree haircut."

"Ana warned Jessie. It'll be fine. Le get her."

Enzo went to his nephew's door. ducked his head and closed his ey eased the door open. "I know you're

Bottom lip curled out, Lorenzo face. "I don't wanna get my hair my dad."

With his arms crossed over his leaned against the frame of the do He looked across the bench seat watching them from the other ded with encouragement. It wo better if she tried to get Loren

"Here's the thing, Lorenz motivated when you found about the most. "Your dad be happy. He asked me to r safe and to not let her get same thing, right?"

You probably don't remember me. I was in fourth grade when you graduated. You helped the coach with elementary PE classes. All the girls had the biggest crush on you."

"Really? Even after he made y'all do a hundred push-ups and run laps?" Resa bit her lip, apparently trying not to laugh.

"Oh, I don't think it was that many, and he did them with us. Of course, he was so focused, I don't think he noticed us gawking at him."

He frowned. "Wait. You're Glenn's little sister. You have four kids?" How was she old enough?

"Yep. All grown up and the mother of four. Our middle ones are twins."

"Now she runs after our little one and lifts them in and out of car seats. It's a workout." Her husband kissed her forehead. The affection between them reminded him of his parents.

"Hi, Lorenzo. I'm so excited you are letting me cut your hair today. Are you ready?"

"Yes, ma'am." He looked so serious. If Enzo could make this little boy's world right, he would in a second. But he couldn't bring Julian home, so he would focus on protecting Ana until the rest of the family could get here.

"Mommy!" A girl of about five stopped in the doorway. "One of the twins peed in the bed."

"Would you mind holding him?" Jessica said and handed the boy in her arms over to Resa. He was already reaching for her. "I'll be right back."

Resa settled him on her hip and he played with the colorful beads on her bracelet.

"Go. Go. I've got him. We can have a chat about all the colors on my bracelet. My favorite is teal. What about you, Adam?"

She smiled and continued talking. Adam babbled some nonsense, but she responded as if she understood every word. She was a natural with kids.

"I'll go inside and get the last few boxes," Scott said.

Enzo pulled his attention away from Resa and the toddler. "Do you need my help?" he asked.

"Nah. They're small. I'll also check on Jessie." Scott jogged back into the house.

Hands on hips, Enzo stood between the house and his Bronco. Lorenzo stayed close to Resa. He didn't blame the kid. With one smile from her, the world was right. She was a safe harbor, a beautiful one.

Narrowing his eyes, he pushed that thought down. He stretched his neck and looked up through the trees and into the sky. The sun had reached the midmorning point, and the temperature was rising with it. "At this rate, we will easily break one hundred."

Adam yelled a response and Resa laughed. She walked toward him, Lorenzo glued to her side. "You look like a guard on duty. Is it a habit, or just who you are?"

He forced himself to relax, took off his aviators and slipped them inside his blazer. "Maybe both." He took a breath and held a hand out to Adam. The baby said something with a tone of utmost importance and reached for Enzo's hand.

The tiny hand barely wrapped around Enzo's callused finger, which went straight into the baby's mouth. Enzo's brow creased, but he didn't pull away.

"We have a chewer." She grinned. Drool dripped as the boy tried to talk.

Enzo lowered his head. "It's not polite to talk with your mouth full."

Adam mumbled more incoherent words.

"That sounds bad." He nodded at the little boy, who stopped chewing and stared up at Enzo with a look so serious Resa suppressed a laugh.

"Really?" Enzo responded and nodded as Adam went back to chewing on his finger. "That happens a lot in life, but you'll be fine."

"What's he saying, Uncle Enzo? I don't understand any of it."

Resa laughed. "Your uncle was always good at languages."

The drool had soaked his sleeve, but Lorenzo had called him "uncle," so it had been worth it.

Scott came back with the boxes, and Jessica was right behind him with three children in tow. "Oh no." Jessica reached to take her son. "I forgot to warn you he is chewing on everything. If he can get it in his hand, it goes to his mouth."

Resa's eyes had totally melted as she watched the baby. She should be a mother by now.

"I've been chewed up and spit out before, so this is no *problema*."

The boy fussed when he lost Enzo. "No. No chewing on people." Jessica laughed. "When y'all get one of these guys, you hear words come out of your mouth that you would never have imagined." Jessica tickled the baby's tummy.

"Lorenzo, come with me, and we can make your mom proud. Okay?"

He turned to Enzo. "You'll be with me?"

Scott ruffled Lorenzo's long hair. "Go ahead and let her shampoo it. Your uncle will be there before she cuts a single strand. But first he is going to help me put your old furniture in his car." He came up behind his wife and laid a hand on her waist. "They warned us that life would change faster than we could blink, but it's all good. Living the dream. You'll see when you start your family."

"Oh no." Resa's eyes went wide. "We—"

But Scott had already turned to the baby furniture and was waving them to the back door. "It'll only take a sec to load this, then he'll be right with you."

Enzo watched until Resa disappeared with Jessica and Lorenzo.

"Nothing more amazing than watching the mother of your children taking care of them. It'll be here before you know it and then you'll wonder what you did with all your time before them."

He didn't bother to correct the man about the relationship between Resa and himself.

They moved as fast as possible to load the crib and other pieces in the back of his Bronco. Lorenzo had called him uncle and wanted him to be there for the haircut. He wasn't going to let him down.

"How long have y'all been dating?" Scott asked as they put the last item in the back seat.

"Daddy! Joel's eating my book!" A cry from

the other side of the door interrupted them before Enzo could deny any relationship with Resa.

"Gotta go. Nice meeting you." He rushed back to the house. "Her shop is right past the back door on the left."

The door was open. Lorenzo looked relieved when he joined them. Had he thought Enzo would be a no-show?

Jessica combed the dark curls back from the small face. "So you want me to use the clippers on the side and then cut the top?"

Lorenzo hesitated, wrapping his arms around his body. Was he about to cry? Enzo stepped up next to him and looked into the mirror to make eye contact. Resa was standing behind them. She would be better at this. Why was he even there?

There was a touch on his hand and he looked down and saw Lorenzo's small hand on his. He flipped his over and gently wrapped his fingers around his nephew's. "That sounds like a haircut your dad would get. Your mom likes his hair, so I think you should go for it."

With too much seriousness for a little kid, Lorenzo nodded. "Yes, ma'am."

Jessica went to work, chatting about the things her kids loved when they visited Port Del Mar. She was fast and didn't take long. Lorenzo never let go of his hand, and she worked around it.

"All done." She took off the black apron and brushed the loose hair away. "What do you think?"

He looked at Enzo. "I think you'll look just like your dad, and your mother is going to love it. She wanted to see those eyes, and there they are." He grinned and then glanced at Resa.

She joined them. "Yep. Your *tío* is right. But don't let him know I said that."

Lorenzo looked confused for a moment, then he leaned forward and whispered, "He's right here. He knows you said that."

Laughing, Enzo lifted their hands so Lorenzo could jump down. "I'm going to need my hand so I can pay her for the great job."

Lorenzo let go and went directly to Resa.

Enzo pulled out the cash Ana had given him and included a good tip. He turned back to Resa and Lorenzo, and the boy held out his hand.

The three of them walked to the Bronco holding hands, Lorenzo in the middle. There was a weight on Enzo's chest that made it hard to breathe.

This was the kind of moment families shared. Lorenzo jumped without warning.

Out of instinct, Enzo tightened his grip and lifted the boy.

Lorenzo laughed and kicked his feet. "Higher!"

They did it a few more times until they were at the Bronco. Resa rubbed her arms. "You're getting so big, I'm not sure I can lift you much longer."

Opening the door with one hand, Enzo gave him a boost into the back seat with his other. "When my dad gets home, he and *Tío* can do it. They're super strong."

Enzo's stomach fell. If everything went as planned, he wouldn't be here when Julian came home. Was he setting expectations with his nephew that he couldn't live up to? The last thing he wanted was to disappoint another person in his life. It seemed all he was good for was being a special agent.

Jessica brought a bag over and handed it to him. "Here's the last of the baby items Ana loaned me. If I'm missing anything, have her call me. Let her know that she and the baby are in our daily prayers." Resa took the bag from him and placed it next to Lorenzo in the back seat.

The incredibly happy mother of four hugged Resa. "It was great seeing you. Ana was right, as usual. Y'all make a striking couple. And you work so well together with the kid." Jessica's voice was low, but Enzo could still hear her. What had Ana been telling people?

She had some explaining to do. He moved to open the passenger door for Resa, but his path was blocked. Without any hesitation, Jessica hugged him too. No one hugged him. She didn't even seem to notice he was stiff. He waited for her to let go.

Over the shorter woman's head, he made eye contact with Resa. She was biting her top lip and her eyes were wide. He narrowed his gaze. Was she laughing at this situation or trying not to cry from embarrassment?

"Y'all make a great couple," Jessica told him. "I love my family, but it unquestionably takes teamwork." Her smile was huge. "You'll find out soon enough." She stepped back, finally, her smile almost swallowing her face. Could it get any bigger? She leaned into his space again. "I know Ana is worried about you, but you picked the best." Her eyes twinkled.

He stepped back. Resa was the best and deserved the best and that would not be him. "I'm not... We are not together."

Her eyes widened and she covered her mouth. "Oh, I'm so sorry. I must have misunderstood. And the way y'all were standing together... Well, it just looked natural. I'm sorry." Her face was red. "Please, forget I said anything. I don't get to talk to adults often." She walked to the garage and then turned around and gave them an awkward wave.

He went to help Resa climb into the Bronco. Who else had his sister talked to? Resa had to be mad or embarrassed.

The idea of family and friends plotting behind their backs had his blood boiling. He would be talking to Ana as soon as he got back on the ranch.

# Chapter Seven

With one hand preventing her skirt from misbehaving, Resa used the other to boost herself into Enzo's Bronco. His gentle touch on her arm prevented her from falling. She managed to mumble a thank-you before he closed the door.

The idea of her and Enzo having a child still had her brain short-circuited. She braved a glance at him as he walked in front of his vehicle. He was his stone-faced self. Nothing fazed him. Once he was behind the steering wheel, he returned Jessica's strained goodbye with an easy wave.

Had he not heard Jessica? Ana was out of her mind. Who in the world would put her and Enzo together? Ana had been the ringleader at putting her ridiculous list of potential husbands together, and Enzo wasn't anywhere on it.

He lived in Denver. Said he was never going to marry again. Actively didn't want kids. Jessica had to have misunderstood Ana. She was dealing with four young children. Ana would never put her and Enzo together.

She nodded as the bizarre situation settled. That was why Enzo wasn't reacting. He knew Ana would never say those things.

Plus, she was so far off his radar that he didn't give it any credence. She was his little sister's pesky friend. She looked in the rearview mirror. Scott and the children had joined Jessica on the driveway. Their little family of six watched as Enzo drove down the tree-lined street. Other families in the neighborhood were starting their day and moving about.

Why did it make her throat burn with unshed tears? Enzo already thought she was flighty. If she cried now, it would just be worse. The edge of her soft pink polish was chipped. Picking at it, she flicked a large piece off.

*Great.* It landed on the back of her hand. Now she would have to remove all the polish. She flattened out her hands and splayed her fingers. Jewelry was not her thing, but she'd always imagined she would be wearing a gold band by now. The ring she dreamed of was never fancy, but sentimental.

Jerking her gaze away from her naked finger, she looked out the window. A young dad was pushing a stroller as he jogged along the sidewalk. Would Darren take his baby out on his daily runs in the local park?

Tilting her head back, she closed her eyes. Darren was not God's plan for her. She'd get over it.

"You're in charge now." Enzo had stopped at the entrance of the neighborhood.

She blinked. "What?"

"Can I call my mom? I want to show her my new haircut."

"Good idea, buddy. There's a tablet in that messenger bag," Enzo said.

Resa handed the bag over, and Lorenzo worked it like a pro and was talking with his mom in no time.

"That was thoughtful of you," she said.

"Just a classic bribe technique from an absentee uncle." He glanced in the rearview mirror. "We're out of time."

Her thoughts were still confused. Her mom and sisters loved to tell her she was running out of time for that big family she wanted. But why was he…?

He tilted his chin so he could look at her over his aviators. "Your cat retrieval."

"Oh." He wanted directions. "Left. Turn left. So sorry.

"I need to text Darren, too, and let him know we're on our way. If we're grabbing something to eat, it will take us a little over an hour."

"I have snacks in the cooler. Not that I can take credit for that. Ana told me what to bring." He glanced at the rearview mirror and a slight smile softened his face.

"Okay, so forty-five minutes." Her hands were shaking as she typed out the letters. The response was instant. "He will be waiting at Hardberger Park, the Blanco entrance."

Wanting to put as much distance between her and Darren, she quickly sat the phone in a cup holder facing Enzo.

"There's a playground there, so that's good. You can take Lorenzo." She checked on the little boy. He was all smiles, talking to his mother.

"We are not leaving you to face the ex by yourself. Until all of us can go to the play-ground, none of us are going. Not until we have the cat and Darren has left the park."

With a sigh, she tilted her head against the back of her seat. In less than an hour, she would be face-to-face with her past and pos-sibly his new family. The family she'd wanted, but he hadn't. What if he had been her last chance at a family? When she'd broken it off, he had told her he could be ready.

No. No second-guessing herself. She didn't want to force someone into something they didn't want. Exhaling a long puff of air, she opened Ana's Fall Festival file on her laptop. She wouldn't think of Enzo and children. No wasting energy on Darren either. Focusing on Ana's health, and helping her friend, was a productive use of her time and energy.

Darren and his life choices were not. She closed her eyes. *Thank you, God, for surrounding me with a wonderful family and friends. Forgive me for my selfishness and complaining about not having everything I want.*

She had so much in her life, why was she wasting time on the things she didn't have? Above the festival file was the list Ana and her sisters had made for her. The list that would lead her to the right husband. The list was proof she wasn't grateful for the blessings she did have, and that she wasn't trusting God with her future.

She glanced over the list of traits of the perfect husband followed by a list of single men they knew. She deleted it. When she got back to the ranch house, she'd throw away the copy Ana had tacked on the wall calling it a vision board. Resa snorted. Maybe they all needed glasses and more faith.

One thing was clear. Darren was her past,

and she wasn't going to let him steal her future by creating fear and self-doubt. She would trust God. That's what she needed to write down and post all over her house. With a quick search, she found the verse that would become her battle cry.

Proverbs 3:5-6. *Trust in the Lord with all thine heart; and lean not unto thine own understanding. In all thy ways acknowledge him, and he shall direct thy paths.*

"You're plotting away over there. Should I be worried?" Enzo broke into her devotion.

Filling her lungs with air, she closed her eyes and stayed quiet for a bit before answering. "No. Just realigning my life with God."

He frowned. "Shouldn't that happen in church or somewhere more sacred than my Bronco on the way to rescue your cat from a spineless ex?"

"It's a perfect time. When God talks, I listen. Any time. Any place."

"God talks to you?" He lowered his head. "Like you hear a voice?"

"Not a voice. More like an epiphany. Out of nowhere, I can get a clear understanding of something I'm struggling with."

"And that just happened? While you were sitting here next to me?" He said it like she had developed a nasty rash.

She laughed. "You know they say God works in mysterious ways. So, yes. Right here in your Bronco on my way to see my ex." She closed her eyes. "Please don't let his pregnant wife be there."

Enzo took her hand, but before he could say anything, Lorenzo spoke up.

"Mommy says she's tired and needs to take a nap and for me to use my best manners. I told her I am. She says I'll get ice cream and that I can play games on the tablet."

Enzo tilted his chin. "And she already hung up before talking to me about this. That sounds awfully convenient."

"It's not awful at all. It's a reward for being good. I'm being good, right?"

She had to grin. "He means that we don't know if you are telling the truth, because he didn't get to talk to your mom."

His small face tightened in a frown, and Resa bit her bottom lip to stop the laughter. That expression was one hundred percent from his uncle.

"I don't lie." He crossed his arms over the tablet. "Mommy said she couldn't keep her eyes open. She had to go. Is she okay? Should we go home?"

Resa reached back and patted his knee. "No.

Your *tío* was just trying to be funny. You can play a game. Do you already have one set up?"

He nodded. "*Tío* made a folder of games I can play. But he hasn't let me play them yet."

With a purposeful glance at Enzo, she tried to get him to say something helpful. He looked at her and lowered his brows. She raised hers in response.

With a sigh, he nodded. "Your mom is fine. Napping is good for her. You can play the games until we get to the park. Are you hungry?"

"No." Lorenzo was all smiles now. With his tablet in his lap, he touched the screen.

Enzo leaned closer to her. "Do you think she's okay? It's still morning. Should she already be that tired?"

Resa was a bit worried, but telling him wouldn't help anything. "She was up early, and she is probably not sleeping well at night. I've told her to get sleep whenever she can." That was all true, but Ana hardly ever complained about being tired.

He nodded as if he trusted her judgment. That was progress.

"So what did God tell you?"

"A scripture was put in front of me. Proverbs 3:5-6. It's about trusting God and not my own understanding. I tend to forget that. I deleted the husband list. I don't need one."

She had said too much. Closing her eyes, she turned her face away from him. Talking to Enzo about her weakness of faith had drained her. On a grown-up conscious level, she knew leaving Darren had been the right thing to do, but there was a part of her heart that wasn't as mature as it should be.

Either way, a nap did sound good. Not that she could actually sleep sitting next to Enzo while he drove her to meet Darren.

She was getting her cat. That was the focus. Princess Leia would be back with her. Life was getting better. God had given her a good life. She just needed to focus on the blessings. Not the unrealistic urge to take Enzo's hand and think about a future with him. She had already wasted too much time on a man that didn't share her dreams, why would she do it again with her best friend's brother.

# Chapter Eight

Had she meant she didn't need the list or didn't need a husband? Not something he should be worried about either way. Enzo reached behind her seat and took a chorizo-and-egg breakfast taco out of the Yeti container. The soft tortilla was still warm. He glanced at Resa. Her eyes were closed.

He was pretty sure she was pretending to be asleep so they didn't have to make awkward conversation. "Resa. We're on Blanco Road. Do you have a meeting point?"

Stretching her arms above her head, she rolled her neck. "He said they'd be at a picnic table in the middle. The playground is a short walk away."

Lorenzo's head shot up. "A playground? Can we go?"

"Once we pick up Resa's cat, we'll go over

there. You can wait ten or fifteen minutes, right?"

"Yes, sir."

He pulled into a parking spot that Resa pointed out. The concrete picnic tables were under a thick canopy of live oak trees. Sun filtered through the branches but most of the area was in deep shade.

Resa climbed out of the safety of the Bronco before he could say or do anything. She scanned the area to the north and then turned south. With a frown, she looked at her phone and typed something short. Obviously, her ex was a no-show.

Enzo helped Lorenzo out of the car, grabbed the cooler and they joined her. "Not here?"

"He says they'll be here in ten. Since he lives five minutes away, that means they haven't even left the house yet." She sighed. "You guys can go over to the playground."

Instead of being happy about that piece of good news, Lorenzo looked up at him with a frown. "We shouldn't leave her alone."

Pride pulled a smile from him. Enzo placed a hand on the small shoulder. "Good call, champ. We'll stay with you until the cat is in your possession, Resa."

A small shift in her shoulders told him she was relieved. It probably irritated her that she didn't want to face this man alone, so he pretended not to notice.

Enzo didn't like the sound of this guy who'd led Resa on for years and then given everything she had asked for to someone else.

The guy wasn't worth any of her time. He hoped she accepted that as a fact.

Restless, he walked to the edge of the trees and back. With a sigh, he stopped at the end of the table closest to the road.

Smirking, she shook her head and turned her attention to Lorenzo. "Your *tío* is walking the perimeter to ensure our safety."

"Should I help him?" The boy tried to speak in low tones, but Enzo could hear him clearly.

"No. I think he likes doing it alone. Tell me what your mom thinks of your hair."

The quiet of nature settled around them. It didn't feel as if they were in the middle of one of the largest cities in the country. Resa seemed to finally relax a bit as she listened to Lorenzo. Bracing her elbows on the table, she leaned back, tilted her chin to the sky, and studied the leaves.

Her silky waves hung loose around her shoulders. She was beauty without trying. The oversize sunglasses along with the bold print of her dress gave off a glamor vibe. He snorted.

Growing up, Resa had been more of the

rough-and-tumble type. She'd been a barrel racer. When she wasn't on the back of a running horse, she'd played sports and raised goats and steers for FFA. She had built her own small herd and sold them to other Future Farmers of America kids to show.

"Do you still have Prince Harry and his ladies?" he asked.

"That question came out of nowhere." She laughed and turned to face him. "I can't believe you remember the name of my billy goat. When I left for college, I sold the herd to one of the Sanchez boys. Prince Harry's descendants are still pulling in top ribbons across the state."

"You had a billy goat?" Lorenzo asked. "I want goats, but Mom says we have enough animals to worry about. I want rabbits too. When I grow up, I'm going to work at the zoo."

"Really." Enzo grabbed the tablet. "That sounds cool. I think there's a zoo game on here." On the opposite side of the table, he set his nephew up with a drink, snack and new game. "You can play while we get Resa's cat. If you're good, we'll go straight to the playground from here."

With a nod, Lorenzo settled in. Reza leaned in close, her scent surrounding him. The breeze caught her loose hair. Fisting his hands, Enzo stuffed them in his pocket to control the urge to push it in place. *No touching.*

A dark red Jaguar pulled into the spot next to their picnic area. "That's him."

They stepped away from Lorenzo as one and went to the sidewalk. He stood slightly behind her even though everything in him screamed to put his body between her and the threat. But this was her fight, he was backup.

The engine went silent. It was a showy ride. He gave a low whistle.

"Don't be impressed. It's a 2008." With a very uncharacteristic high-pitch laugh, she glanced over at Enzo. "He got it for ten thousand dollars and spent that amount on polish."

Long, graceful fingers fidgeted with the neckline of her dress. One of the nails had a large chip missing. Had she been picking at it? Without question, she was nervous. He stepped closer and her breathing eased.

The driver got out of the muscle car. His brown hair had perfectly placed highlights. Were those Armani shades? This couldn't be her ex. In a million years, he would never put down-to-earth, laughing-out-loud Resa with sleaze like this guy.

The man came to the front of the car and smiled at Resa. "It's good seeing you. You look great." He twirled his keyring around his index finger. Mr. Cool just stood there for a while, staring at Resa. He never even acknowledged Enzo.

A short woman with cropped blonde-and-pink hair struggled to get out of the passenger side. She stood and adjusted her long white T-shirt, pulling it down. The graphic tee had a logo he didn't recognize, but it was stretched tight over a very extended belly. The bottom hit her midthigh. Right above high-heeled leather boots. Very urban.

She walked around to the front of the car and put her arm through Darren's. Even with the heeled black-leather boots, she couldn't be over five four. It was too warm for all that leather to look comfortable, and he'd be surprised if she didn't deliver within the next month.

After a few moments of silence, the woman leaned forward and extended a hand to Resa. "Hello. I'm Kimberly. Darren's wife. You must be Rizzo. Thank you for taking the cat. They're so dangerous to newborns." She rubbed her belly and gave them a smile that didn't reach her eyes. Okay, so she was going to try and play power games.

Enzo smiled. Resa wouldn't fall for that immature bait.

"It's Resa," Darren snapped. "I told you a hundred times."

Resa nodded. "That's okay. I love the name Rizzo. And, about cats… A lot of people believe that, but it's just a myth. Not true in the slightest. But I'm happy Darren called. It's exciting to have her back." She turned back to Darren. "Where is Princess Leia?"

He tossed his keys into his seat and turned to the opening tailgate of his coupe. He disappeared behind the hatchback for a while and then joined them. A small pink-and-brown crate was in one hand, a large canvas bag in the other. Poking out of the top was a ball with a feather dangling off a string. A horrible yowling sound was coming from inside the crate.

With a small distressed sound of her own, Resa rushed to the crate before Darren reached the front of his car. She took the crate and lifted it to her face. "Hey, Princess Leia. I've got you, baby girl." The cat answered in an authoritative meow, sounding a little calmer.

Kimberly stepped back. "Careful. She'll claw and bite. That cat is a menace."

"She is not." Darren glared at his wife. The cat gave a long-suffering cry. "You've made it clear from day one you don't like her. How else do you think she'd respond?"

"She attacked my ankles from under the sofa."

Ignoring them, Resa took the crate to the table opposite where Lorenzo sat. The game no longer had his attention; his gaze darted between Darren, Kimberly and Resa. All her focus was on the cat. She kept a smooth line of soft words flowing.

Enzo moved closer to Lorenzo and placed a hand on his shoulder. Hopefully, that would be enough to reassure him everything was okay.

Her ex stepped away from his wife and followed Resa to the table. "Listen, Resa. I'm so sorry." He apologized several times without being clear about what he was apologizing for.

Was he sorry about the cat? Or that he got married less than half a year after she'd left him? Maybe he was apologizing for not being a man Resa deserved. Either way, Enzo had no time for him. He was trying to figure out how to shield Resa from this guy without causing more trouble.

She blocked him with her shoulder and then sat on the end of the bench. Resa didn't need him. With the crate on the table, Resa unlatched the door and eased her hand inside.

"I wouldn't do that," the wife warned. "It was almost impossible to get her in that thing. Darren has scratch marks to prove it. She's dangerous. It would be best to turn her over to animal control." Kimberly pressed herself close to Darren, preventing him from sitting down. Her hands were wrapped around his arm in a death grip.

Ignoring them all, Resa lowered her face to the door. Princess stuck her head out, scanning the area, her ears alert. She paused with one paw out and then lunged from the crate and into Resa's arms. Lying flat, the white-and-black cat curled around Resa's neck, burying herself under Resa's hair.

The yowling turned to a soft, sad meowing. "I know, baby girl. It's okay. Momma has you." The love she had for the cat was visible, and it looked as if she might cry.

*No. No.* Enzo wanted to yell at her. *No crying.* His heart thumped a little harder and he prayed she didn't. He'd made a career of being detached, but it was hard after being back on his family ranch.

He'd do anything to keep his sister and mother from crying, and Resa had apparently joined their ranks somehow.

"That's your cat? She seems scared." Lorenzo scooted down until he was across from her.

Enzo moved to put himself in a better position to shield her, Lorenzo and the cat from the spineless ex.

"She is scared, but it's going to be okay." She

smiled at Lorenzo. "Once we get to the house, I'll let you pet her." With a kiss on top of the cat's head, she eased her back into the crate.

Enzo placed what he hoped was a comforting hand on her shoulder. "Are you ready to head over to the playground before we head home?"

That got him a hard glare from the other man. "Um, I was thinking we could go to lunch, Resa," Darren said. "Your favorite Mexican restaurant is less than three minutes away."

There was a gasp from the petite woman clinging to him. "I have my doctor's appointment in an hour." Kimberly responded before anyone else had the chance. If looks could kill, everyone in the park was in danger.

With a clicking sound, Darren rolled his eyes in disgust and pushed her off his arm. "I don't have to go with you to all of them. I'll drop you off at the house and take Resa and…" He turned to Enzo with a furrowed brow.

"Enzo." Using his low, firm voice, he stared the guy down. He was being pushed to his limit, and that was hard to do. The coward was a piece of work. Did he really think Resa wanted to spend time with him at a table, chit-chatting over guacamole and salsa?

"Yeah, right. They came all this way. I

thought it might be nice to take Resa and… Enzo…along with his son to lunch. There's some…um…things I need to say to her…for closure."

"He's not my dad." Lorenzo sounded offended.

"No." Resa's voice left no room for arguing. "We *are not* going to lunch. I came to pick up Princess Leia. I already have a lunch date with my two favorite men."

"Oh, a date? With him? I thought he was just your ride." Darren swallowed and licked his lips. His gaze stayed on Resa except for a quick side glance at Enzo.

"Thank you for Princess Leia. We have nothing else to talk about."

"But I really need to talk to you. It's…it's important." His little wife was glaring at him, and her skin was turning a brilliant red.

Resa stood. "Nope. We're never talking again. Delete my number. Focus on your wife and child. Princess Leia was our last connection." She turned away from Darren. "Y'all ready for the playground?"

His nephew nodded but still looked concerned, clearly not understanding what was going on.

Darren wasn't done. "Resa. I." He glanced over at his wife then back to her. "Can—"

"No." She took Lorenzo's hand and her long strides ate up the parking lot. She didn't look back. Darren started after her, but Enzo blocked him. "You're done. You have a wife. Go to her."

An engine roared to life behind them. Darren's wife was driving his Jag out of the parking lot. With an overly fake smile, she waved and moved forward. Darren stared at his taillights and then spun around to go after Resa.

"Don't." Enzo stepped in front of him. It was alarmingly satisfying to finally get to do what he had been longing to do since the dude had stepped out of his car. "You have a wife to take care of." He nodded to the car that was at the stop sign a few yards away.

Darren groaned. "Kimberly!" He rushed to the car and banged on the window. After a little begging, he opened the door and slid inside. The tires squealed as they peeled away from the intersection.

Without another thought of Darren and his wife, Enzo jogged across the parking lot and caught up to Resa and his nephew. They were at the gate of the playground. Lorenzo let go of her hand and ran to the climbing wall.

Enzo rested a hand on her stiff back. "Are you okay?" Probably a stupid question, but he couldn't think of anything else.

Resa nodded and moved to a bench. With her head down, long waves of brown and soft copper hid her face. She gently pulled the now-quiet cat out of the crate and cuddled her closely.

Keeping an eye on Lorenzo, Enzo sat next to her. He wanted to wrap her in his arms, but that was a bad idea. "You did great back there. I hope you realize you made the right choice leaving him and coming to Port Del Mar."

She continued to pet the cat. It still clung to her shoulder. Resa didn't say anything, but there were a few suspicious sniffles.

"On the way back, let's stop at one of my favorite roadside cafés, Jr's Roadkill Café." She still didn't say anything.

"Lorenzo said he's never been there. We can take Princess Leia's crate in, so that's not a problem. I mean…she will be in the crate, not just take the crate." He waited for a response to his joke. Why was he the only one talking? It was a bit surreal.

He hated chatter.

Reaching out, he touched her shoulder. "Resa. What do you want to do?"

She looked up. Her lashes were soaked. Without a sound, she had been crying her eyes out. His heart broke for her.

Dejection was written all over her face.

"I want to go—" She swallowed. "I want to go ho—" Before she could finish the sentence, she leaned into his arm and let out a huge sob. One hand grasped his biceps and the other cradled her cat.

Her whole body shook with each sob.

*No. No. No. No crying allowed.* That was the rule. This was not good. Not knowing what to do, he pulled her against his shoulder.

With his free hand, he stiffly patted her back. Princess Leia's big green eyes stared at him. Accusing him. It was as if the cat expected him to do something.

He frowned at the cat. *What can I do?* Great, now he was mentally talking to a cat. He didn't like this feeling of not knowing what to do; it was one of the very few times he was lost. There was no protocol or plan of action, that he knew of, for a sobbing woman after seeing an ex.

Lorenzo was swinging from the top of a bar. He laughed as another kid joined him and they raced. Each kid dropped before they reached the other side. Dusting themselves off, they ran to the rope ladder and took off again.

Enzo scanned the area. There were a couple of moms with strollers sitting on the bench. Other than that, it was all clear. Except for the crying woman in his arms.

This was a new danger zone. Looking at his track record, he wasn't successful with upset women. Why were Resa's tears creating a tightness in his chest? This wasn't good on any level for either one of them.

# Chapter Nine

Squeezing her eyes shut, Resa fought to get control of her body. Her head throbbed, her chest burned and her gut hurt. There was no sense of time. How long had she been soaking Enzo's jacket? She had no memory of ever crying so hard. It infuriated her that it was over Darren. He was the last person who deserved her tears.

Worse. It had happened in front of Enzo. More like, all over the poor man. This emotional upheaval wasn't fair to him. Or poor Lorenzo, who was already dealing with too much uncertainty. Trying to take a deep breath, she only managed to make an awkward hiccupping sound. She had to pull it together before Lorenzo saw her.

Enzo had one arm around her shoulder and the other awkwardly patting her back. This was hard for him. He didn't have a history of dealing well with overly zealous emotions. Withdrawing from his comfort, she leaned against the arm of the metal bench to put more space between them.

Princess Leia stayed curled around her neck, and her soft pink nose touched Resa's wet cheek. "I'm okay."

Another hiccup interrupted her breathing exercise.

"Are you sure?" He reached next to him and unzipped a really fancy cooler. He handed her a water bottle. "Drink." Then his gaze went to Lorenzo on top of a fort.

"That must come in handy as a special agent."

"What?" He looked at her for a brief moment, confusion etching in his brow.

She had a feeling he had developed that just for her.

"Always being on guard and prepared for anything."

His features tightened for a moment before reverting to the usual stoic look. "We all get it wrong sometimes."

She wanted to ask questions, but his closed-off face was back, so she took a long drink of the cold water he had given her. He pulled a cloth from his pocket and she used it to wipe her face. It helped.

Putting a little water in the cap, she held it in place for Princess Leia to drink. "I'm so sorry for losing control like that."

"It happens." He hadn't looked directly at her. He brushed at his now-wet jacket and took it off. Twisting, he laid it over the cooler at his feet and then watched Lorenzo as if his life depended on it.

Her cat sniffed her again and meowed. With a sigh, she rubbed her under the chin. The purring started. It vibrated through Resa's chest, easing the ache. "I missed you too."

"How did he end up with the cat?" he asked casually and then gave her a quick glance that probably looked a bit panicked. "You don't have to—"

She smiled. Poor man. Was afraid of getting too personal or that she'd start crying again. "No. It's fine. And just to be clear before I tell you this story, these tears are not for Darren. They're for the loss of a future I thought I had."

Resa stroked the silky hair down the small cat's back. "We were on IH 10 and there was a tiny black bump in the center of our lane. Darren passed right over it and then hit his brakes. He said it was a kitten. I didn't believe him. He pulled off to the shoulder. Another car straddled her. Once it drove past, I saw the little head pop up. Hardly able to walk, she started for the side of the highway, but another car came and she froze again.

"With his flashers on, Darren put his car in Reverse until we were lined up with her. I think others figured out what was going on and started moving into the far lane. A huge dually truck stopped right in front of her and put their flashers on too. It became a little rescue mission. I opened my door, grabbed her and we took off. The other cars honked and waved."

Resa touched the sweet little face looking up at her and stroked a black ear that was missing the tip. "It was a sweet moment that gave me hope for the human race."

"So Darren has moments of not being self-absorbed." He nodded as if missing pieces of a puzzle had been found. A puzzle he didn't like.

She rubbed Princess Leia's ear. "Both ears were damaged and her nose was bleeding. One eye was swollen shut. Large patches of skin were scraped raw and her back leg was broken. Of course, she was scared, dehydrated and covered in fleas. We took her straight to Darren's vet. They kept her for a week and, for the first few days, we didn't know if she would make it. Darren went to visit her every day after work."

He raised his eyebrows in disbelief. She had to laugh. "It's true."

Her fingers soothed the fur on the cat's back. Darren had seemed perfect in the early days. "When we started dating, he'd had a huge orange cat. He was devastated when she passed at fourteen. I know the man you met today seemed shallow, but he loves animals. That was one of the reasons I hung on for so long. I truly believed he would be a great father and would eventually change his mind about kids." She turned to look at the playground. "Well, I guess he did."

She hugged Princess Leia so she wouldn't cry again. "Since he was in a house, and I didn't know where I was going to live, we thought his house would be the best place for her. She loved sitting in the front window. When I left, I didn't want to move her, and I thought he needed her more than I did. So, I agreed to let her stay with him. I knew if nothing else, he's good to his cats. Spoils them."

Enzo scratched under the tiny chin. "She's a survivor, and he's not all bad. Most people aren't. You were right not to stay with him if you had different desires for your life."

Flopping her head back, she closed her eyes. "I thought if I just gave him more time, but one year turned into four. It was always someday with him. He liked having a girlfriend. Being part of a couple was convenient, but he didn't see himself married with kids.

"That's what he told me over and over. But I didn't believe him, so I waited. This opportunity with the birthing center came up in Port Del Mar. It was an open door I couldn't ignore. I had dreamed of a job like that as much as I had of being a wife and mother. Darren wasn't going to help me realize one dream, so I fulfilled the other."

He gently squeezed her shoulder. "Today, seeing him with the cat, the wife and a baby on the way… It was a perfect storm. It hurt to see her with everything you had waited for that he wouldn't give you. It would be too much for anyone."

She looked into the depths of his coal-black eyes. How did he do that? How did he make her feel as if her messed-up emotions were rational? Sitting up, her cat rubbed against her and gave a soft meow. "That's an understatement. I really thought I was completely over him. *I am.* That's why I'm so upset with these stupid tears. I know he's not worth them. But, really? What's wrong with me that in just a few months he gave her everything I waited around for years to get from him?"

"You're the better person and didn't force him into something he didn't want. Being upfront and dealing with it is better than avoiding conflict and letting resentment boil under the surface."

"That sounds like you're speaking from firsthand experience." She searched his eyes, but he turned away and focused on the boys jumping from plastic rock to plastic rock. His face had turned back to stone. Clear message. Discussion about him was closed down.

"Enzo." She reached out to touch his arm and he shifted away from her.

"Lorenzo's been running all over the place like a wild man." His gaze went to his nephew. "It's a suitable time to head back and check on Ana. I don't trust her to follow orders. She's always been a little headstrong."

Too much sharing for today. They fell back into their normal relationship. She smirked at him. "The best of us usually are."

He snorted. Both their phones rang. His was a standard buzz and hers was a happy raindrops-and-rainbows tune.

She frowned. "It's Ana." She answered with it on speaker. "Hello? You're on speaker with Enzo and me. Lorenzo is playing in a fort."

He put his phone away and glanced at Lorenzo again.

"Oh, good." Ana sounded out of breath. "I feel like I'm having contractions. Nothing big or painful. So don't freak out, Enzo. With us being so far out of town, I want to make sure we are safe. I'm having Seth drive me to the hospital to see if I'm in labor."

"You're having the baby? It's too early." At that moment, Enzo did not in any way resemble his calm, steady persona. He turned to her. "I should have stayed with her."

"Enzo, I said no freaking out."

"I'm not freaking out. I just need to know the plan. We shouldn't have left town. We're almost two hours away."

"That's why she is going to the hospital. Just in case." Resa asked Ana a few questions and then turned to him. "She is paying attention to her body, and if she goes early enough, there is a good chance they can stop the contractions if that's even what's happening. It might just be her body adjusting."

"Thank you, Resa. Tell Lorenzo I'm just going to the hospital to make sure his baby sister is good. I don't want him to stress out even more. There is no telling how long they will need to keep me in the hospital. Enzo, please think of this as a fantastic opportunity for some uncle and nephew bonding time."

Enzo looked like he might be sick. Resa wanted to wrap him in a hug but didn't think he'd welcome her comfort.

It would be more productive to focus on her friend's well-being. "Ana, we've got this end covered. Don't give us another thought. I'll call Doc to check in, so don't worry about updating me. You just rest. We'll be there to pick you up when you're clear." They disconnected.

Enzo stood. He looked lost. "What do we tell him?"

Resa stood next to him. "It's time to go home. He'll be hungry. After we eat, we should know if there's anything to tell him. Best-case scenario, Ana will be home for dinner and he doesn't have to know. If she has to stay, we'll explain it to him then."

Unable to stop herself, she stepped closer and placed her hand on the back of his upper arm. "There's no point in worrying about what we can't control. It doesn't help."

"True. We need to look at what can be done." His gaze shifted down to her.

He was back in his default mode, cool and detached. "What happens if she is in labor?"

His obsidian eyes held her, and their depths pulled her under. He hid so much in the shadows.

"Resa?"

Her lungs suddenly filled. Had she been holding her breath? Forgetting to breathe was not good. "Sorry. I was processing."

*Sure, girl.* She was on the verge of seeing Enzo as human. That would be dangerous for her. He was so emotionally shut down and he was leaving soon. It would be a very bad idea to start having feelings for him. Maybe there was something wrong with her. She was only attracted to men who would never commit to her. She pulled air deep into her lungs through her nose.

"Is it bad?" Just looking at his features, nothing seemed wrong. But when she looked into his eyes, she saw what she hadn't seen before. Fear.

"If she is in labor, it's good that she's going to the hospital this early. There are things they can do to stop her progressing. There's all sorts of stages that this goes through, so right now we just need to find out what we're dealing with before we make any plans."

With a nod, he moved away from her and started walking around on the sidewalk where Lorenzo was playing.

At the edge of the playground, he stopped. His jaw was set. "If they stop the labor, will she come home?"

"Remember I told you we need her at thirty-six weeks to safely deliver at home. She is almost thirty-four. If she is in labor, they will keep her there even if they can stop it. At thirty-six weeks, if the baby is not stressed, she can come home."

"Why would she do that? The hospital is safer."

She twisted the corner of her mouth. He was scared for his sister, not doubting her expertise. "Right now, it is, and that's why she is there. But delivering at home is just as safe once she reaches the right time. But she can change her mind. We'll work as a team to make sure they have what they need."

The look he gave her was still full of doubt, but then he turned away from her and clapped his hands. "Lorenzo? Time to go."

His nephew paused. Then he reached for the bar above him and moved away from them. Enzo called again. His voice firmer. Nothing.

She clapped. "Lorenzo Gruene Flores Hernandez. You heard your uncle. *¡Ven pa'ca!*"

The boy jumped from the structure and turned. He waved goodbye to his new friend and ran to her.

Enzo's lips were in a tight line.

Was he mad at her for stepping in and getting Lorenzo? Or was he upset at Lorenzo for responding to her after ignoring him? The small body slammed into her and hugged her. "Can we go see my mom now? I want to show her my hair."

She glanced up at Enzo. Should she say something? She didn't want to make it worse. He looked down at them. His gaze bounced from her to his nephew. Then he looked up to the clouds overhead and sighed. So many muscles were involved in the simple act of rolling his neck.

It was as if he were preparing for a task that would take all his mental and physical strength. Looking at her, he gave her what she assumed was meant to be a reassuring smile. She was not assured of anything.

"Lorenzo, when I call, you come the first time." With deep breath, Enzo dropped to his haunches and balanced on the balls of his feet with arms casually draped over his bent knees. "Do you know why I called you to come to us?"

He wasn't going to give the boy a chance to claim not to have heard him.

Lorenzo looked up at her then at his uncle. "Because you wanted to leave."

"Do you know that for certain, or are you guessing?"

He twisted his mouth and thought about his answer. "I'm guessing?"

"There might have been an emergency, or something wrong, and I needed you to come straight to us. Ignoring me is not acceptable. You know I'm an FBI agent, right?"

He nodded.

"Our response time is important to keep everything on track and all my people safe. When I call you next time, you'll come as soon as you hear me. Understand?"

"Yes, sir."

Enzo held out his fist. "Give me a fist bump." When the small fist tapped the large knuckles, Enzo popped his thumb up, and Lorenzo did the same. Then they went back for a double tap. "That's just for us."

Lorenzo gave his uncle a tentative smile. They looked so much alike.

Enzo stood. "Does Miss Princess want to check out Jr's Roadkill Café?"

"It's Princess Leia," Lorenzo corrected his uncle.

She had to laugh. "You are so much like your uncle."

Lorenzo frowned. "I'm just like my dad." Then he leaned over to peek inside the crate. "She's asleep. Is it okay to move her?"

"Yes. She'll be fine." She picked up the crate, tucked it under her arm and held her hand out to Lorenzo.

"You hungry, Lorenzo?" Enzo asked as they made their way to the Bronco.

"Yes, sir. Are we going to the place you told me about?"

"Jr's Roadkill. I can't visit Texas without stopping there. Not sure what I love more, the brisket or the homemade sausage."

A smile stretched her lips. The first real one all day. "For me, it's the creamed corn and potato salad."

"Um…no. Nonmeat items are not allowed to be your favorite at a world-famous barbecue place."

"Too bad, because I'm not changing my answer. And I'm not sure Junior's place is world famous."

"You cannot rightly call yourself a Texan with that attitude."

She laughed. With a casual shrug, she grinned at him. "Either way, you agree that we must eat at Jr's Roadkill Café. I can't believe Ana has never taken Lorenzo. I've failed at my job as godmother and you've failed as uncle. We must protect him from this sort of neglect."

Enzo nodded. "Lorenzo, Jr's Roadkill also has the best hot dogs the great state of Texas. I know how much you love hot dogs."

Lorenzo scrunched his nose and climbed into his seat with Resa's help. "Roadkill? They make their hot dogs out of roadkill?" He looked disgusted and intrigued at the same time.

"Your great-grandfather, Abuelito Jose, hit a deer once and we put it in the back of the Bronco and took it to the ranch to process. He said we don't want to waste the good life of the deer and need to respect God's gifts."

Lorenzo twisted to look behind them to where the baby gear was now stowed. "There was a dead deer here and you ate it?"

"Uh…" The awkward hesitation was something she had never seen from Enzo. He was trying so hard to make this right for his nephew. She gave him a little thumbs-up to encourage him. His shoulders fell and his look of gratitude over such a small gesture was kind of sad.

"Abuelito Jose was from Mexico, and he was taught to never waste anything."

"So they eat animals from the side of the road at the restaurant?"

"No, no, it's just a joke. Their hot dogs are beef and elk. It's my favorite."

"What about their fries? My friend Thomas, at school, gets fries and pizza made from cauliflower."

As Enzo turned onto the ramp and merged onto the highway, he placed one hand over his heart. "To be an uncle of worth, I pledge to you that I will always serve you French fries made from potatoes and pizza with real bread crust."

Lorenzo rewarded him with a huge smile.

Resa made sure to catch Enzo's gaze and give him a little nod. He was making progress.

"We should take some home for mom to eat. Can't wait to show her my hair. Do you think it makes me look like Daddy? That will make her happy, right? I hope it doesn't make her remember how much she misses him. Then she'll cry. I don't want her to cry."

Enzo lost his cool-and-collected look. Time for a distraction. Resa twisted to see Lorenzo. "Crying can be good for us. It helps get the stress out of the body."

Lorenzo was looking confused, and his poor uncle was uncharacteristically a bit wild-eyed. He looked at her as if she was about to spill all the drama.

Princess Leia meowed.

*Good timing, little lady.* She took the cat out of the crate. "Do you want to see if she will sit in your lap?"

"Yes. Please." Lorenzo swung his feet and then stopped. "Sorry. I should be still, so she feels safe, right?"

"Yes." Holding her arms out, she waited to see if the cat would crawl back over to Lorenzo. He sat very still. The stillest she had ever seen.

"Hello, kitty. Come sit with me." He lowered his voice like she had done. Princess Leia took a careful step from her and made a small jump to land on Lorenzo's knees. "Look. She likes me."

"What's not to like?" Enzo chimed into the conversation.

"Stephanie at school says I'm a know-it-all. She doesn't like me. But that's just because she is bossy and wants everyone to do what she says." The cat nosed Lorenzo's chin and meowed. He giggled. "Can she stay here with me?"

"She can stay as long as you are both happy."

Enzo glanced at them using the review mirror. "If she wants to come back to Resa, let her go. I don't want you getting scratched up by a mad cat."

"She never gets violent."

"Darren's arms and wife tell a different story."

"That's not Princess Leia's fault. They were going to drop her off at a shelter. Animals know when people aren't nice."

"I'm nice." Lorenzo tilted his head and rubbed his cheek on her head.

"Yes, you are. If you happen to do something she doesn't like by accident, her ears will lay flat."

He nodded. "It's a tell. Mom says animals

and people have them, and we have to watch for them so we don't annoy them without meaning to. Sometimes I talk too much or too loudly. I move around a lot too. Mom says some need stillness. I have a hard time with stillness."

"We all have something we need to work on. But that thing can also work in our favor when we use it right."

"What do you do that annoys people?" he asked his uncle.

Resa bit down on her lip, but her laugh must have escaped before she closed it all down. He looked at her, one brow quirked, and cleared his throat.

"I have been accused of always following rules and taking the fun away from other people. I'll analyze a situation, and if it is dangerous, I make decisions without emotion. In a personal relationship, I come across as cold and uncaring, but at work it makes me good at what I do." His jaw locked down. The muscles were flexing.

He was upset about something. Before she could ask, Lorenzo leaned forward.

"Mom says you care more than you let us know." He looked at the cat. "Thank you for taking me to the playground. It was so much fun, and I have a new friend. His name is

Cody. He says I should come back, and we can play again. He has a baby sister. She's too little to follow him on the playground. I told him I'll have a baby sister soon, so it'll be a long time before we get to play together. I hope I won't be too big to play with her."

He finally took a breath. "Look. She's asleep. Can I play that zoo game?"

Enzo looked a little shell-shocked. He turned to Resa and shrugged.

She nodded. "Of course. It's there in the pocket outside that cooler."

Once Lorenzo was engaged with saving the endangered animals, Enzo leaned slightly toward her. "He's going to hate me. I don't see any way we can have a good outcome un-less…" He glanced over his shoulder. "Un-less everyone is home when we get there." He straightened and sighed. He didn't like not being in control.

"God has this. In Second Corinthians and Romans, we are reassured that we can trust God in grim times."

"How can you have that kind of faith? Bad things happen all the time."

Her heart tightened. There was no way of knowing the things he had seen in his line of work. "The Bible tells us it doesn't come easily, but we must have faith that He ultimately works it all to the good."

He tilted his head back as he stared down the highway.

Resa fought the urge to reach over and take his hand. Her faith gave her so much peace. She wasn't sure how she would survive if she didn't have it to comfort her. Enzo deserved that kind of peace too.

She knew without a doubt she was way too emotionally invested in a man who would leave. Her chest hurt with the knowledge that her heart would be broken all over again. Why did she do this to herself?

# Chapter Ten

Halfway through his chili cheese dog and fries, Lorenzo collapsed against Resa. He had fallen asleep midword. Enzo had never seen anything like it.

Gently, she stroked the boy's hair back with such longing in her gaze that it hurt to watch. Confounded by the way her ache for a family affected him, Enzo turned away.

Once she was done eating, he went around, picked up the sleeping child and carried him to the Bronco. It almost felt natural. And that was a little terrifying.

One wrong decision could ruin a life forever. He wasn't sure he deserved Lorenzo's trust. Ryan had trusted him. The rookie was now in a coma because something had gone wrong during the raid. Enzo had been the lead. Every step they'd taken had been planned by him, was his responsibility.

Leaning into his SUV, he adjusted Lorenzo into the booster set and buckled him. He took a minute to put the superhero blanket around him. Enzo tucked an extra strip of material against the window to cushion the small head.

Like he had a million times since that night, he allowed the minute-by-minute timeline of that last mission to play through his thoughts. How had Ryan ended up alone in the back office? Where had Enzo gone wrong? He closed his eyes. Just like all the other times, he didn't see anything new. What was he missing?

"Enzo?" Resa pulled him back to the present. "Are you okay? She's getting the best care. My gut tells me it's going to be all right."

He stepped away from the warmth of her hand and opened the driver's door. "I'm fine. I got in my head for a moment trying to figure out another problem."

Her eyes searched his. For a cold minute, he barricaded all emotions and allowed her to study him. He needed her to know he was fine. His walls were cracking.

Not able to hold her gaze any longer, he turned his back to her and climbed into the Bronco. Hands on the wheel, he waited until she was strapped in and had the cat settled. He should have gone around and helped her, but his restraint was weak. The more distance between them, the better.

Why did she bring so many emotions to the surface? They were easier to deal with the deeper they were buried. Of course, his cynical side pointed out that it made it easier because he *wasn't* dealing with them.

This was not a conversation he was going to have right now. Putting his brain and all stray thoughts in lockdown, he shifted to look over his shoulder and backed out of the parking spot.

They were quiet as he merged with the traffic on the highway. The only sound was the wind at the windows and the soft snoring from the back seat. Resa pulled out her phone and was texting. He locked his jaw. Once she gathered all the information, she let him know the status of his sister.

His body ached from all the tension he was holding on to. It was all this pointless emotion trying to break the surface. It just needed to stay down.

They were almost at the ranch and she hadn't looked up from her phone. He was about to break his silence and ask for an update when she put the screen facedown and looked at him. He gripped the steering wheel tighter.

Leaning across the console, she put her hand

on his. "Relax." She patted him and then gave the back of his hand a gentle squeeze. Everything about her was gentle.

"I'm sorry." She was whispering. "I was texting with a few different people, and your mom was asking questions. If I looked up... Well, you were quiet, so I oiled the squeaky wheels. Not that they are..." She blew out a puff and air and rolled her eyes. "I'm making a mess of this. Sorry I made you wait so long."

"Is she coming home?"

"Your mom or your sister?"

"Either. Both would be great."

Her generous mouth disappeared into a tight line.

Dread gripped his gut. He would be alone on the ranch, fully responsible for his nephew. How was he going to do this? "Will Ana be coming home soon? What about my parents? What did my mom say?"

He was too old to need his mother. But right now he felt like a nine-year-old home alone for the first time, and it wasn't going well. He wanted his mother.

"Doc was there, and they admitted her to the hospital. The good news is they were able to stop the labor and her water didn't break, but she had started dilating."

"Dilating? That's bad. It means the baby's

coming?" *Breathe*. The brain needed oxygen to function at full capacity. He knew that.

"It means her body is getting ready, but a woman can walk around for a month dilated one or two centimeters. With her history, they're going to keep her in the hospital just to be safe."

Another deep breath. "Okay, so what's the plan of action? What do we do now?" Lorenzo was now his responsibility twenty-four hours a day. Along with running the ranch and ensuring all ninety-two heifers birthed their calves safely.

*Oh, and don't forget the Fall Festival*, a tiny sarcastic voice laughed in his ear. Really? He shook his head. "I need a plan of action." He glanced at his nephew who was still peacefully sleeping in the back seat. He was not going to be happy with the news.

"We have to tell Lorenzo." He glanced at Resa. She looked composed and ready to tackle whatever came their way. Their way? Were they a team now? He couldn't believe this, but he really hoped so.

He'd never imagined a world where he would turn to Resa Espinoza for help, but here it was. "Did my mom give you a timeline for their arrival at least?" *Please let it be within the week*. Was that too selfish to pray for? Probably, since he had not uttered a single prayer of thanksgiving or praise in several years.

She nodded. "It looks like the earliest your parents will get relief so they can leave is in three weeks, maybe two. Ana has a little less than two weeks to be in the safe zone. If she can make it, they will let her come home because the baby will be full term."

A sweat broke out over his entire body. He was going to be alone. What if he failed? "I don't know if I can do this." He exited the highway.

Resa looked confused. "Do what?"

"Be responsible for Lorenzo and the ranch." Then there was all the organizing and planning for the festival. How did his sister do everything and take care of her son? "When the little man back there finds out his mom is in the hospital, he's not gonna want anything to do with me."

"I imagine he will be upset at first, but we'll talk him through it. I'm right across the driveway. Just like we organized the Fall Festival into chunks and sections, we'll make a working plan for the ranch. You're not alone. There is a whole community that is waiting to help you. Lorenzo will be fine. His mom will be home in a blink of an eye."

"How can you say he'll be fine? All he has

right now is me. I'm in no way equipped to care for a child."

"Enzo, during the week, he will be spending a good chunk of time in school. I can come over in the morning and help him get ready and feed him and take him to school on my way to work. You'll be able to start early to tackle any ranch work that needs to be done for the day."

"I don't even know where to start. Ana was giving me a list each morning."

"Okay. I'll come over for dinner, and we can make a list of everything to do for the next day. If we aren't sure, Ana is just a phone call away. Lorenzo can ride the bus home, which should give you enough time to get the chores done. If there are days that the work goes later, my sister can pick him up when she gets her daughter. That's what she did for Ana. Your sister doesn't do it all alone, and neither will you."

There was a knot that lived in his stomach lately. He couldn't afford to make any mistakes. This last year had been littered with one failure after another. Miscalculations, misunderstandings and errors haunted him. The perfect world he had worked so hard to build had collapsed this year, and he hadn't seen any of it coming.

For most of his life, he'd known what he wanted and gone after it. He had worked hard, and it had always paid off. Was he now paying the price for the wins?

It had been so easy to judge others for not performing to his expectations, but now it seemed as if he didn't have the skill set to fix his problems.

Like his marriage. It had ended before he had known there was a problem. Then there was Ryan, fighting for his life because something had gone wrong on a mission Enzo had been in charge of.

No one had called to give him an update. That meant no change, good or bad. Maybe right now was not the best time to be responsible for his nephew.

Resa's hand touched his arm. He wanted to lean into her warmth. *No.* He stiffened and pulled back slowly, hoping she wouldn't notice his reaction.

He was so deep in his own head, he wasn't paying attention. Dangerous. He should always be aware of their surroundings. What was he doing?

"Enzo, she and the baby are going to be fine. I want you to visualize a month from today. Your parents are home, and your sister is holding her new baby daughter. The ranch will be fine, and the Fall Festival will be an enormous success."

Great. She was using the same voice on him she had used to calm her wild-eyed cat. He wanted to resent her for treating him like a child or wild animal, but it was working, so he opted not to say anything. That was always a sound option.

She leaned back into her seat to check a text notification, and he wanted her back close to him. A clear sign he was not in his right mind. He had no business wanting to be close to her. Needing her was bad.

"It's your mom."

Hope flared, but he shut it down. Hope led to disappointment.

"She says to tell you to stop overanalyzing everything." Looking up from the screen, she smirked at him. "You might not come home much, but the lady knows you."

He gripped the steering wheel. His parents deserved his honesty, and all he had given them the last year were lies. The knot in his gut caught fire.

"She wants me to remind you that you don't and can't control everything. God has us each where we need to be if we are in prayer." She reached over and touched his arm. "Have faith."

They were at the gate of the ranch. He paused and crossed his arms over the steering wheel. "What does that even mean? She's needed here, obviously." The gate was open? Had they moved the herd to the back pastures, or had they been in such a rush to get Ana to the hospital that they'd forgotten to close it?

"Our mothers share the same faith."

He looked over at her. "Do you?"

She gave him a weak smile. "For the most part. I have moments of weakness, but I find comfort knowing that God is bigger than any problems I face." She looked down and grinned. "She said to tell you, and I quote, 'Romans 8:28. And we know that all things work together for good to them that love God, to them who are the called according to his purpose.'"

"But what about all the people running around not loving God?" He shifted the gears and drove through the gate. "I'm going to close the gate in case they just forgot and there're cattle still in the front pasture."

She nodded.

He scanned the area for any evidence of escaped cows. It looked clear. He didn't want to be the one to lose cattle. His goal was to hand the ranch back over to his sister the way she'd left it.

He had a gut feeling his mother would be sending Resa Bible verses every day to read to him. He slipped back into the Bronco and shifted gears.

He could feel her eyes as she searched his face, saying, "Your mom's right about being where you need to be." He forced his jaw to relax. His gut told him she saw too much. "Call your parents. Talking to them might help, but you can do this."

She leaned away from him, crossed her arms and grinned. "I mean, come on. You organize missions to rescue people. You spend time negotiating with bad guys. I realize I'm oversimplifying what you do, but my point is you manage a really complex job that requires good people skills."

How did he explain that it was exhausting for everyone to see him as perfect? His mom blamed Brit for the collapse of their marriage, and he didn't know how to tell her it had been all his fault. Then there was Ryan. Enzo had been responsible for some random mistake that might still kill the rookie. He hadn't received any word about the investigation and wasn't sure if that was a good thing or bad.

At the house, he cut the engine and stared at the wide-open horizon dotted with a few barns and cattle.

"Enzo." Resa shifted. Real concern was stamped all over her face. "You know, your family brags about how fast you were promoted and how great you are at your job. You're highly skilled and successful at whatever you try. You qualified for state in swimming after only one year on the team. I do believe you can do anything. You can do this ranch thing with your eyes closed. I don't think I've ever seen you doubt yourself. Is there something else going on with you?"

"No." *Well, that sounded too sharp and defensive.*

She pulled back and her mouth tightened. Great. She was being all friendly and supportive, and he'd shut her down. There was a burning in his chest and he forced himself to admit he was going to need her.

He took a deep breath and scanned the wide horizon past the house. "There was." More than he could apparently deal with.

It felt as if his life as he knew it was over. But he wasn't used to sharing. Would she side with Brit or see his side? Did he have a right to be bitter that his wife hadn't bothered to tell him she was unhappy until she'd been caught with her *friend*?

Would it help if he opened up and said something about Ryan? Or would she only confirm his fear that it was all his fault. Up until this last year, he had gone through life with a false belief that he had it all under control.

"We're home," Lorenzo's sleepy voice yelled from the back. His new haircut was flat on one side and stood straight up on the other. He was reaching for his seat belt. "I can't wait to show Mom!"

It was time to shake off this funky mood. His family needed him to be proactive. He glanced over at Resa, hoping she had the right words. "We are out of time." His voice was low and raspy to his own ears.

She took Enzo's hand. This time he didn't pull away.

"Hey buddy, we need to talk. Resa got a message from your mom."

The worry popped up in his nephew's gaze. "What wrong?"

Resa squeezed his hand. One deep breath. "She's good, and your baby sister's okay, but they had to go to the hospital to make sure they stay safe. The doctors are there to help them."

The little guy lost all the coloring in his face. "I told you I needed to stay home." The cat looked up at him and blinked her big green eyes. Lorenzo petted her. "We left her alone." His voice was lower now, so as not to scare the cat. "I want Daddy. Daddy should be here. He'd keep them safe." His small fingers were buried in Princess Leia's thick fur. With his head down, he started crying.

Enzo opened the door, jumped out of the Bronco and moved to get his nephew, but once he reached the boy, he wasn't sure what to do.

Resa was twisted in her seat, patting his leg. "She's safe. Let's get in the house, and I'll see if we can talk to her." She gently took the cat and put her in the pink crate.

Enzo reached for his nephew, but Lorenzo pulled away from him. "No. I hate you. It's your fault." He pushed at Enzo. "Go away so my dad will come back."

"Here. Take her." Resa passed the crate to him and turned to Lorenzo. "Come here. There is no need to blame your uncle. He's just trying to help. He loves your mom too."

Lorenzo leaped into her arms and muffled something against her neck. She nodded and rubbed his back. "Your mom and sister are getting the best care."

With a sympathetic look to Enzo, she headed to the front porch. There was nothing else to do, so he followed.

Once inside, they went to the kitchen table. Resa texted Ana to make sure she could take a call from them, and Enzo set up a video call on the tablet so they could see each other.

After saying hi, he stepped back to give

them space. He stood in the archway between the kitchen and the family room. Lorenzo sat in Resa's lap and chatted with his mom before hopping down because he wanted to show her something in his room.

Resa stopped and stood next to Enzo. She hugged him. No one hugged him. "Relax. It's just a hug. We all need a good hug every now and then."

With a smile, he found himself relaxing. He slipped his arms around her shoulders and kind of hugged her back.

"See, it's nice," she whispered. "It's going to be okay."

He wanted to believe her. He did. The contact was nice. Maybe if he could stay here on the ranch with Resa, he would eventually feel like his old self. But was that what he wanted? Could he trust himself to not destroy her light?

In Resa's hug, the world fell into place. But it was an illusion. He knew that better than anyone.

She moved away, taking the warmth and reassurance with her. Her hand went down his arm and she took his hand into hers.

"Remember, he's just scared." She squeezed his fingers. "You had a great day and made so much progress. You'll be his favorite uncle again by morning. You'll see."

"I'm his only uncle." But he got it. He was scared too.

Lorenzo's voice floated down to them. He was sitting on the stairs telling Ana about the cat.

"I'm going to unload the furniture and then go check on the stock," Enzo said.

Ana had left him a short list of things to do today, so it was a good excuse. Was he hiding and avoiding? Probably.

He looked at his watch. "I'll be out late. Can you stay with him? Stay for dinner." He hoped it came across casually, but he wanted to beg her. His pride just wouldn't let him go there.

"Of course. Lorenzo likes helping in the kitchen, so that's a great way to keep him distracted. We'll make biscuits. The garden and chickens need to be checked. We'll be busy, and dinner will be ready around eight thirty. It's a late dinner. Does that work?"

"Sounds perfect." He headed to the back door and Resa followed him.

"Resa! Don't go!" Lorenzo ran from the stairs and tackled her. One arm clutched the tablet closest to him, the other wrapped around her in a death grip.

She dropped to his level and cupped his face. "I'm not going anywhere. You and I are going to make dinner for Tío Enzo while he gets some chores done."

"And you're going to stay the night?"

"No. But I live on the other side of your driveway. I'll be here first thing in the morning to start you and your *tío* off on the right foot. While your mom is resting in the hospital, we are going to work as a team to make sure she doesn't worry about the ranch. We need your *tío*. Your mom needs him."

He nodded but didn't look happy about it. "I want Daddy. He'd fix everything." He leaned into her again. Wrapping him in a hug, she gazed up at Enzo. With just one look, she reassured him that everything was going to be okay.

He grabbed his old hat that had been hanging by the door as if waiting for his return. It still fit. He wasn't sure why that surprised him, but it did.

On the other side of the door, he paused and looked back. Resa had Lorenzo on her hip. They were looking at the tablet and talking. His nephew had a smile on his face. She kissed him on the side of his head and he giggled. They didn't need him, but he knew as much as he would like to believe otherwise, they were becoming essential to him.

Enzo's heart heaved into his gut at the

thought of leaving and not seeing them every day. But what choice did he have? His life was in Denver. Their life was here in Port Del Mar.

For now, he would fill in the gap. And when his parents and brother-in-law returned, his life would go back to normal.

Why did the idea of them coming home and him being free to get back to Colorado feel so heavy? It should lighten his mood.

Pulling the old hat down low, he closed the door and went to the barns.

# Chapter Eleven

Resa took the last washed plate from her sister-in-law, Lilianna, and placed it in the cabinet. They had stayed in the kitchen to clean up the last of the family's Sunday lunch. It had been a week since Ana had moved to the hospital, and they had fallen into a nice routine on the ranch, but she still couldn't figure Enzo out. At times, she felt like he saw her and valued what she did, but then he would be all cold and standoffish.

Lilianna bumped Resa with her shoulder as she pulled coffee cups down. She had been part of the family since childhood and was now married to Resa's brother, Bridges.

"You missed last Sunday's family dinner, and I haven't seen you. Tell me how it's going with you and Enzo. I heard you had a road trip together last weekend. From the sound of it, you won't be needing the list we made for you. I was surprised we haven't seen Enzo at church."

Resa groaned. Dinner had been going so well. Why had she believed they wouldn't have the conversation about her love life? Talking about the ranch would have been a safer option. She hadn't been able to stop worrying about her boys all evening. *No.* She was worried about Lorenzo. His uncle was just the man taking care of her best friend's son.

Last night at dinner, when she had asked if he and Lorenzo were going to church, Enzo had been noncommittal. She hadn't wanted to get too pushy, so she'd backed off. Now she wished she'd offered to take Lorenzo. Routine helped keep things as normal as possible. Not to mention fellowship and prayer were important in times of uncertainty. What was Enzo thinking?

She knew faith was not a priority for him, but she had hoped he would at least follow Ana's routine when it came to taking the boy to church.

Why did he make it so hard to understand him?.

Her sister-in-law bumped into her again and grinned. "He has you lost in thought. Um, this might be bad." She grinned. "Or good, depending on the outcome."

"I'm not lost—"

"I asked you several questions. You didn't hear a word, did you? So, spill. How bad do you have it for him? I personally think you make a cute couple."

Six kids of assorted sizes ran from the living room through the kitchen. The screen door slammed behind them. *"¡Camina! ¡No corras!"* her mother called after them, but they were already gone.

*"Momi,* I don't think they know how to walk," Bridges said as he carried his new daughter into the kitchen and kissed his wife on the forehead.

"You would think they were raised in a barn." Resa's four-foot, eleven-inch mom shook her head. "Those boys of yours have too much energy."

"I'm pretty sure it's not just their boys." There were more than thirty people over for her mother's Sunday lunch, and a little more than half of them were under the age of twelve. It made for a chaotic but fun afternoon. She usually loved this.

Resa poured a cup of fresh coffee and went to the side table to pick a sweet to eat. Or three. Her sisters owned a bakery in town, and they always brought something home for the Sunday meal.

"Don't think I didn't notice you not answering my question," Lilianna said as she filled her plate with a pink *concha*, two *elotes* and a *pan de muerto*.

Resa followed suit and made a mental note to take some of the grilled corn and sweet breads to the ranch for the guys. They all went out to the patio, where most of the women had gathered to eat their sweets.

Resa shrugged. "I'm just helping out while Ana's in the hospital. You know Lorenzo is a great kid, but he can be a handful."

Her sister Josefina came up on her other side. "I told Margarita that you should have gone to them after church. You had a thing for him as a kid, and now you're both grown adults. He's a good man. You could do a lot worse if you're looking for a husband."

"I did not have a *thing* for him. And I'm not sure I'm looking any longer." She said that just as there was an unusual moment of silence in the normally noisy gathering.

Kids came and went as they needed something from their mothers. She was the only one without children. Her and her youngest brother, Reno, but he didn't count. No one expected him to settle down for a long time, if ever. He claimed a relationship would dampen his fun. She worried he would never grow up. Their mother seemed to enjoy and encourage his childishness. He was the youngest of seven.

For years, Resa's main goal in life had been to be a mother and wife. The kind of dream that had to have a partner.

"You don't like the list we made for you?" Selena De La Rosa asked. She was the mayor of their little town, married to the oldest De La Rosa and mother of triplets.

"No, it's not that. I just think, maybe I need to be more open to what God wants from me. Not everyone has the purpose of marrying and having children."

Many of the people around her sat back and stared at her with raised brows. Most of them were related to her.

Josefina cut a *concha* in half and gave it to her daughter, who then ran away again. She shook her head. "Nope. Everything was fine until Enzo came to town. Then that slimy ex called and you heard he has a wife and a baby on the way. You have a right to be upset. It's all too much, so you're claiming that you don't want a husband, but we all know you do." She plopped a piece of pink bread into her mouth.

"Enzo Flores would make a perfect husband for you. Now that he's back in town, I can see why you would throw out our list." Belle De La Rosa grinned. "I get it."

"No—"

"You know he drove her to San Antonio to get her cat back from Darren. Ana said he didn't want her to face Darren alone. Wasn't that sweet?" her mother said.

She opened her mouth to try again. "N—"

"Enzo comes from a great family. His parents are on a mission trip in Peru, and he came home to help Ana. I'm sure he's ready to stay. He's been gone so long," her oldest sister, Margarita, added.

The conversation was all about Resa, but they wouldn't let her get a word in. "Look at Bridges. He told us over and over he wasn't moving back. Now he's married with kids and living down the street."

"Hey. Keep me out of this," their oldest brother yelled as he rocked a baby.

His wife, Lilianna, swatted him playfully and then leaned forward. "So you spent the day together and you live next door. Have you gone on an official date?" Her eyes brightening, she straightened. "Wait, how did the date with Steve go? I'm assuming not well since you are tossing the list."

"I heard Steve didn't work out so well and Enzo came to your rescue." Jazmine, her client and friend, joined in with that bit of information she must have gotten from her husband, Elijah, who owned the Painted Dolphin and had seen the wreck of that date firsthand.

"He rescued her from a bad date. How romantic is that?" Josefina smiled.

Everyone who knew Enzo from school started sharing their favorite memories of him. She tried to say something, but it soon became an avalanche of Enzo and Resa stories. Everyone acted as if they had been the cutest couple in grade school instead of playground nemeses.

Her phone rang. Since she was with all of her family, it might be a client. It could be Ana. She stood as she looked at the screen. It was Enzo. Her heart kicked up a notch.

"Hi, Enzo." She walked away from her family. "Is everything okay?"

A deep, masculine chuckle was her answer. "That, Resa, is a loaded question. I'm calling because I think it's best if you come and get Lorenzo."

She had her back to her family, but they were uncharacteristically quiet. Taking a few steps around the side of the house, she asked, "What's going on?" Had Enzo lost his patience already?

"We went out to ride through the north pasture, and on the way back through the large barn holding the heifers, I spotted one separated from the others. She's in labor and looks like she is struggling. It might be normal labor things, but I didn't want to traumatize Lorenzo if there is a problem. I don't think he should have to handle that with everything that is going on with his mom."

"I agree. I'll be right out."

"Thank you." The relief in his voice was audible.

Tucking the phone away, she returned and faced her family. She had never wanted to escape her family so much. "I need to go to the ranch. There's a problem with one of the laboring heifers."

"You're going to help with a heifer?" Her brother arched an eyebrow.

"What does that mean? I've helped Dad, and I deal with labor for a living."

"Don't listen to him. He's just messing with you." Her sister stood. "I'll go with you and take my daughter. We can keep Lorenzo distracted, and you can help Enzo. That's what he needs, right?" Josefina was moving to the door. "To keep the poor boy from any birthing trauma?"

Enzo probably didn't want to think about birthing heifers right now either. He had called her to help. Why did that make her heart flitter?

The poor man needed help, and her number was the only one he had. That was all. She was also a midwife and he wanted free labor advice.

Her heart couldn't afford to read into his innocent actions. No matter how much she wanted some of the things her family had said to be true. He wasn't interested in her.

Even if he was, Enzo had made it clear he was going back to Denver as soon as his parents crossed the threshold of the ranch house.

# *Chapter Twelve*

"They're here!" Lorenzo ran out of the barn. Enzo had loosened the horses' girths, keeping them ready so Resa and he could head straight back to the north field barn.

She had sent a text to let him know that Josefina and three of the kids would keep his nephew busy. She offered to go with him to check on the new mom. That had released some of the tension from his shoulders.

The group came to meet him at the barn doors. Lorenzo was the happiest he'd seen him since he'd heard the news that his mother was in the hospital. "*Tío*, can I show them my new game?"

"Sounds good. I'm going to take Resa out for a ride to see the cows."

"Okay. Cool." He ran to the house with his friends. To have that kind of energy again.

Josefina waved at him, raised a plate covered in foil, and then followed the kids.

Resa went into the barn. "My mom sent dinner over."

"Wait. The house is—"

"Locked? I figured. I gave her my key. I told her you prefer the house to stay locked at all times." She grinned at him. And for a moment he could breathe. She was so perfect on every level.

She raised and eyebrow. "Are we riding?"

"Yeah, we can cut straight through the pasture. It's faster than taking the road past my grandparents' place." He gathered the two horses and handed her the reins of the palomino mare Lorenzo had been riding. "Are you okay with her?"

Resa rubbed the mare's muzzle. "Ms. Sassy and I go way back to when she was actually sassy." Gathering the reins, she swung up onto the horse like a pro. "They should call her Mellow Yellow now."

He mounted the big sorrel that was his dad's favorite, Lone Star Arrow. The leather creaked under his weight. They were just a few feet apart as they cut through the house pasture. He hadn't known how uncertain he was until she'd suggested going with him. "Thank you for coming. I appreciate your sister coming out too. I didn't want Lorenzo to be upset by something he can't control."

"I agree. I'm glad you called."

He took a deep breath. They passed the old homestead and the barn was in view. "Ana said it would be another two weeks before they start calving. It's a good thing we finished baling the hayfield early and brought the first-time moms closer."

"That was smart. You never know what you get with the first-timers."

Her compliment made him ridiculously happy, but he hoped he played it cool. "It's been a long time since I dealt with laboring heifers. I don't want to lose any on my watch." Restless energy boiled inside him. Needing to move out, he leaned forward and pushed his horse into a lope. She followed.

There was a comfort in having someone working with him. Especially Resa. There was a solid confidence she would handle any emergency with grace, calmness and quick thinking.

He frowned. Since when had he thought of Resa as anything other than the girl who got his sister in trouble? Shaking off the uncomfortable thoughts, he slowed his horse down and entered the barn.

They left the horses just inside the barn

doors. The large open stalls had runs with sliding walls the size of garage doors pushed back. Most of the young heifers stood outside at the hay feeders. Some were chewing on baled alfalfa.

He took a deep breath. The rich earthy smell of the sweet hay calmed him. He hadn't known it was his favorite aroma until this week when he'd helped Seth stack it.

At the far end of the barn and in the deep shadows in the last stall, the first-time mother was still breathing heavily. "There she is. Looks like she's moved around a bit." The straw bedding was tossed in a circle around her.

Resa passed him on the way to the stall. For a moment, the black heifer tried to get up, but her legs wouldn't hold her.

Resa opened the gate and, with slow, careful movements, she went to the animal's head and petted her neck. "It's okay, girl. We're here to help."

He leaned over the railing. "When I saw her struggling, I quickly checked and didn't see if her water had broken. But I was in a rush to get Lorenzo back to the house. We had a good day, and I didn't want to ruin it with the trauma of a difficult delivery. I wasn't expecting this."

"Life is like that. That was about twenty minutes ago?"

He nodded.

"Then let's give her another thirty. The more she can do for herself, the better."

"I called the vet. She's on standby if we need her."

Resa nodded as she ran her hands along the heifer's rib cage and examined her.

"Ana should have some coffee stored in the supply room she tries to call an office." With the sun going down, the warmth was leaving the air.

"Coffee sounds good. You didn't happen to bring any of your sisters' sweet breads?"

"I did, but they are back at the house. Sorry."

"I'll survive. More importantly, I want to make sure these two make it through the night. Ana needs to trust me to take care of things so she doesn't have to."

"We can gather up any of the supplies we might need. It will be easier to have everything ready in case we need it." She gave the solid black heifer a few more reassuring words and then came out to join him. Her fingers flew as she pulled her hair into a side braid. "She is fully dilated, and her water broke. So, if something doesn't happen in the next thirty minutes, we'll check her and see if pulling the calf will help. Right now, I can't tell if we are dealing with a breach." She used the rubber band that had been on her wrist to tie off the end as she talked.

Enzo lost all appetite for any sweets. "That will be a call for the vet."

She nodded. "Yep. We don't want to try that on our own."

They found the coffee and he started a pot. Resa was going through stacks of folders on the desk. "Oh good. Here it is. A list of everything that could go wrong and the actions to take."

"That sounds like fun reading." He found a couple of cups and washed them in the utility sink.

"Being prepared for anything is better than the alternative. I love a meticulous checklist." She read through it and scanned the large wire shelves on one wall. "It's organized by tubs." She pulled a large tub from the middle shelf. Clean OB Chains and Handles was printed clearly on a large white sticker. "Good. They're clean and ready to go if we need to pull."

He got a little queasy. He was fourteen the last time he'd been in the calving barns and his grandpa and dad had had to pull a calf. They had lost the mom. He hadn't been much help that night. He'd gotten sick. That might have been around the time his dad had stopped lecturing him about his responsibility to his heritage. Ana had been a natural. She had done whatever had needed to be done without a moment's hesitation. His father had probably been relieved that he'd had at least one child who had inherited the ranch gene.

Resa was going through the shelves and putting a few items in a small canvas bag. She looked like she knew what she was doing.

"Have you done this before?" he asked.

She nodded as she scanned the shelves for something else on her list. "I used to go out and help my dad. It's weird, but I knew from that moment that I wanted to work in labor and delivery." Standing on her toes, she stretched to reach for a purple tub labeled OB Gloves, Lubricant and Rags.

He stepped up behind her and reached for it easily. She turned to look at him, placing her between his arms. They were so close, yet they weren't touching. Her lips parted to say something, but they both froze. He hadn't been aware of a woman in a long time. Why now, and why Resa Espinoza?

His lungs forgot to work. The long lashes that framed her tiger eyes lowered in slow motion.

*Kiss her.*

The order was being yelled somewhere in his caveman brain. He wasn't sure how long they stood there staring at each other as if finding a new species.

Clearing his throat, he stepped back. "Here." He handed her the box.

"Thank you." She turned and looked around the room as if lost.

Had she wanted him to kiss her? This wasn't good for either one of them.

"What else do we need?" If they stayed focused on the problem at hand, the awkwardness would disappear.

"There should be items that we'll need if the calf isn't breathing."

On the bottom shelf by the door was a bucket. Written in bold Sharpie were the words Ice Water and Straws. For as much grief as he gave his sister for being too spontaneous and flighty, he was impressed with her level of organization. "When did she become queen of labels?"

"When her husband wasted time looking for stuff because she was the only one who knew where everything was. Right after she had Lorenzo, Julian was out here trying to do all this without her. As soon as she got back on her feet, she had it done. She's done a great job of keeping the system going." She waved to the desk. "Her paperwork, not so much."

He laughed. "It would worry me if she became an uptight neat freak in all areas of her life."

"Only one per family?" she asked.

Growing up, he'd lectured them over and over on the merits of keeping everything in its place. He humphed. "That's probably more than enough for everyone's peace of mind."

After they set up the boxes a few feet from the heifer, they went back and found a couple of camp chairs. Hands on hips, she looked over their haul and scanned the laminated list. "All we need is iodine. I'll go get it."

"When did you become the follower of lists? First, one for the perfect husband, and now this. If I remember correctly, you hated lists and rules more than my sister."

Instead of getting annoyed and snapping at him, Resa laughed. That surprised him.

"Right? But to be clear, the husband list was never my idea. That was my tribe trying to fix me up. But, like your sister, I've grown up and have found a use for a well-thought-out list. Especially in an emergency. Darren hated any kind of list or long-term goals. He wanted to live in the moment and take any path open to him. He claimed to be too free to live by a list. It was fun at first."

"Sounds more like a lack of maturity to me."

She turned her back and looked at the heifer. "That's probably true. As I've gotten older, I have found value in creating lists. A fragment of your million lectures must have worked its way into our brains." She moved back, plopped in the red collapsible chair, and propped her boots on the middle rail.

For a moment, Enzo just looked at her. There was something about her that made him want to stay right there and watch her. Listen to her. She was more than beautiful. How had Darren not given her the life she'd wanted? "My guess is that your ex resents being told what to do." He stretched the accordion legs of his chair and tapped it on the ground to ensure it was structurally sound before easing into it. He wasn't completely certain it would hold him. "People like him don't understand the importance of rules. Rules are in place to keep society running smoothly."

"Now see what you just did." She waved her arm in the air as she rolled her neck over the back of the chair.

She made him wait as she looked at the beams above them. "We find common ground about lists and my ex, and then you knock us off the island. I'm not too much of a rule follower. People breaking society's rules created some of the greatest moments in history. Jesus worked on the Sabbath. The leaders didn't like His radical thinking at all."

Another finger came up as she ticked off her points. "The Declaration of Independence. Women being arrested because it was illegal for them to vote. Sometimes rules are just put in place so a certain group can keep their power."

With sigh, she turned to him. "Don't get me wrong, there are some good rules, but how can we explore life and all its possibilities if we are tied to a bunch of random rules someone else made up?"

She was all excited. It was fun to watch her light up, so he leaned closer and said, "You're contradicting yourself. Rules and lists create structure. Law and order. They go together."

With a gasp, she shook her head.

"What? You had a list of men you are supposed to date?" He frowned at her. "Sounds like rules and order to me."

"There were no rules. Just a guideline to keep me focused on my goal of having a family. My sisters and Ana were just trying to help. They know how much I wanted a family. Truthfully, it had more of my sisters' prints all over it." She looked back up at the beams and shrugged. "It wasn't a bad idea. I don't have time to waste if I want that family. Darren had some good qualities, and I kept clinging to those even after all the warnings that we were not on the same page when it came to life goals. I thought he'd eventually change. My mistake. Finding reasons to stay because it's less scary than being alone. I was playing it safe and by the rules. Maybe I should revisit the list."

His gut twisted. He did not want her to consider anyone on that list, but is wasn't his business. It was time to change this unsettling topic. "You being a midwife makes perfect sense now. They're rabble-rousers."

Her mouth fell open. "What? No! We are respected professionals and were helping women way before there were medical doctors."

Grin suppressed, he raised a brow. "That's true, but then doctors took over and made new rules. They pushed the midwife out of the picture and claimed to be the experts. The hospital was the only safe place to have a baby."

He pointed to her. "So modern midwives come in and reclaim your spot, breaking down the system that was in place for several generations. Fighting the man. You rebel."

Squinting her eyes at him, she tilted her head. "I can't figure out if you are mocking me or making a good point."

"Why does it have to be only one or the other?"

Her braid slipped over her shoulder as she shook her head. "I hate to admit it, but part of what you're saying might be right."

He cupped his ear and bent closer to her. "What did you say? Did I hear agreement that I'm right?"

A snort was her only reply. She leaned back and studied the overhead beams again. He waited for her to start talking. "When people question you all the time and accuse you of putting mothers and babies in danger, it wears you out. Then there are the ones who think it's all touchy-feely with no substance. But midwifery is so much more than that. It's about giving power back to women. Obviously, I'm not anti-hospital. Right now, that's the best place for your sister and the baby."

Enzo opened his mouth to say he was just messing with her, but the words didn't make it out in time. She was blinking fast. Too fast. Like, trying-not-to-cry fast.

No clue what to say at this point, he took a sip of coffee and watched the heifer for any changes. Now would be a suitable time to do something. How could he distract Resa?

"What's on this husband list they made for you?"

*Really, circling back to the list? Was that the best his brain could do?* He didn't want to explore the strong emotion that bubbled in his gut at the mention of her going back to her list for her husband hunt.

He would be gone soon, and she deserved the life she wanted. A life he would never be able to give her.

The breathing of the heifer was the only sound between them. Had Resa heard his question?

"A man of faith that wants a family. I grew up in the middle of seven children and, for the most part, I loved it." She made a strangled laughing sound. "That might have terrified Darren. He was an only child."

"You want seven? I think that would freak most men out."

"At my age, I am not having that many unless I have two sets of triplets. That's not happening."

He shrugged. "You never know. More bizarre things have been known to happen. You could always adopt."

"I've thought about adopting as a single woman, and it's on the table. It might be the best option for me." Her voice was sad; there was a longing in it that pulled at his heart.

He didn't know what to say or do. The conversation needed a ninety-degree turn. They lapsed back into silence. The desire to promise her that she would have everything she wanted pushed at his chest. He wanted to soothe her, but it would be an empty promise, and he never made a vow he couldn't keep.

He fell back, letting his head rest against the back of the chair. Breaking a vow even unintentionally tore at him. Brit had not felt cherished or loved. Those had been the promises he had made to her. Ana would never forgive him if he broke Resa's heart.

Raising his head, he looked at her. "If you want four kids, you have the persistence to make it happen. Growing up, my mom told us over and over that God puts the desires in our hearts, and it is up to us to carry them out. It's what Mom told my dad when I was determined to leave the ranch and join the FBI."

"What if I was meant to have kids but the man I was supposed to have them with made the decision not to have any." She crossed her legs and picked up a piece of straw, twirling it.

He stood, walked to the railing and looked at the timer on his watch.

"Maybe I can help with your list…you know, from a man's perspective."

"He has to be serious about settling down. And tied with that, he must be a man of strong faith. He must live in or want to live in Port Del Mar."

"I see why I was cut before I even knew there were tryouts."

"Did you want to be on the list?" She joined him at the railing with a smirk on those pretty lips.

*Yes.* "No." He scoffed more at his inner voice than her. "So this is a strict checklist. I thought you were more of a romantic. What about letting yourself fall in love?"

Opening the gate, she checked on the heifer. "Did you see where that got me? I thought I was in love, and I was willing to wait. I thought compromise was important in a relationship."

He followed but kept his distance. "It's not a compromise if one person is giving everything up for another. That's a lack of respect."

With a heavy sigh, she moved through the gate "Maybe I was just being greedy. I have a career I'm passionate about. I get to help other women. That's a great purpose and should be enough." She walked around to the other side and went to her knees next to the heifer. "Oh, there's a hoof."

He came around in time to see it disappear. He looked at his watch. "We're not in the danger zone yet, and if I remember correctly, that's normal."

"Yes. She's not in distress, and the calf isn't breech. We'll give her a little more time."

Twisting away, Resa had her back to him. She lowered her head and rubbed her brow.

"Resa. What's wrong?"

With a resigned huff, she stood. "Nothing. Just time. Instead of trusting God, I panicked. The idea that I was running out of time created a deep fear of being alone. I made bad decisions. Fear is not from God." Arms crossed over her middle, she looked to the horizon.

He took a step toward her, laying a hand on her arm. For a moment their gazes connected, and he wanted to say so much. But it would be lies. He wasn't staying.

After a long moment, she pulled away, went outside, and walked through the small group of young cows.

The heifer pushed again and the hooves and nose appeared. He checked his watch. "We'll give a bit more, but you're running out of time, momma. It would be so much easier if she could just tell us what she needed." He looked for Resa.

Resa had left him. She stood outside with her form silhouetted as the sun balanced on the horizon. He had never felt so useless in his life And that was saying a great deal after this year.

He stayed near the heifer. A part of him wanted to go to Resa and wrap her in his arms and promise her it would all work out. But he knew better than anyone that sometimes good people didn't win.

He stayed near the heifer. He could help her and in doing so help his sister. That's why he was here.

# *Chapter Thirteen*

Resa had a million thoughts and emotions running through her head. Enzo had pointed out things she had never thought about. The heifers were settling in for the night. She ran her hand over their extended middles. The hair was soft but coarse at the same time.

"Resa?" Enzo was behind her, still in the barn standing guard.

Taking a deep breath, she straightened. "Don't worry. I'm not going to lose control again and get everything wet. I'm in my own head and wondering what I did wrong that she did right."

Enzo shook his head. "He is married to her and expecting a child because she manipulated him in ways you wouldn't."

She frowned, not understanding Enzo's point.

"Describe Scott's reaction with his family the other morning."

"Are you going all FBI on me? He was around six feet with dark blond hair. She was—"

"No." He chuckled. "Not the physical descriptions. How did the man interact with his wife and children? What expressions, words, actions, did you notice?"

Twisting her lips, she briefly closed her eyes to replay the interaction with the family. "They were loving. He casually touched her and kissed her cheek. He had a nice smile. Even when the kids seemed to need a lot of attention, he appeared genuinely happy. He's a man who loves his wife and family." The kind of family she always imagined having.

"I agree. Did you see that in the next couple we saw that day?" He couldn't say the man's name.

Closing her eyes once more, she shook her head. "He got into a situation he didn't want and now he feels trapped."

Enzo nodded, ran his hand along the back of the heifer and then stood next to her. "Let me make a guess, and you tell me if I'm right. When you broke it off and told him you were moving back home, he offered to marry you and even set a date. I imagine he promised you would have children in the near future. Whatever you wanted if you would just stay."

In shock, her gaze darted off the resting heifer to Enzo. "How did you guess that? He did all those things."

"He's easy to read. He wanted to keep everything the way it was, but he didn't want to lose you. You, Teresa Espinoza, would never emotionally blackmail someone to get what you want. Not everyone has that kind of integrity. In my experience, that type of decency is rare in today's world."

"Your sister would never do that, nor would any of my siblings. Our parents raised us better than that."

He grunted in reply. That first night she'd seen him, the darkness and coldness in his eyes had been deeper than she remembered it in high school. He had gone out to be a hero to the world at large. But at what price? "I'm so sorry that's been your experience."

He shrugged, as if the loss of his innocence was inconsequential. "Without knowing them, I'd guess that the pregnancy was a surprise to Darren but not Kimberly."

Resa almost felt sorry for him, almost. She took a moment to pray for that innocent baby thrown into the middle of the drama. "The Radcliffe family in San Antonio is the dream. Working with women, I've seen it too many times. Wives and mothers pretending everything is good when inside they're desolate. That's not the kind of relationship I want. I'd rather be alone."

She sighed and walked back into the barn. "Mom always told us that God is powerful enough to bend us to His will, but He wants a true relationship. He waits for us to come to Him willingly. That's what free will is all about. That's the kind of love God gives us. He's there waiting, but it's up to us to agree. To surrender."

Free will.

Enzo stood next to her as they stopped at the threshold of the stall. She was drawn to him. He made her feel safe and centered. But it was all wrong. It would be the same thing all over again if she let those feelings grow past this new friendship they had found. "Do you think you'll ever want to move back to the ranch or have a family?"

"No." His answer was fast and sure. "My life is the FBI. There is no room for a family in that. Not a happy one."

That was her answer. She had known what he would say, but it still hurt to think he would be leaving. She was too tired to think about ever dating again.

He cleared his throat and turned to her. "Sometimes I—"

A loud bellow from momma cow interrupted him. She had all their attention.

The calf played peek-a-boo with them. Enzo reset his watch. "It needs to happen soon, or we have to intervene."

With a nod, Resa agreed. She lost track of time over the next ten minutes or so as they waited to see what the new mom needed from them. Enzo brought the tubs and bags closer. He set out the chains.

She really didn't want to use them, and if she read Enzo correctly, he didn't either. "It's been too long. The time to help her—"

The heifer grunted and, after so much struggle, the calf easily slid into the world right at Enzo's feet. The long black legs bumped his boots. He dropped to his haunches and then stood and took a step back. "We need to give it time to stand, right?"

"Yes." The calf wasn't moving. "But she's not breathing." She checked its muzzle. Enzo dropped to his knees and laid a hand over the narrow rib cage.

"I need the suction." Without hesitation, Enzo jumped up and was back with the bulb and rags. He wiped the face.

"Do you want me to add another scoop of ice to the water?"

She didn't take her focus off the calf. "That's a good idea. Bring the bucket over here."

The bucket and all the other tubs were within her reach in less than a minute.

Enzo was back and dumped a scoop of ice into the bucket with the partially melted ice water. She finally glanced up at him. His jaw was set.

"You know CPR, right?" she asked.

One sharp nod and he was on his knees with the small body between them. She laid her hand over the little heart that should be beating. "Do the compressions right above here."

It felt natural working with Enzo. It was smooth and easy.

She used the straw to tickle the little nostril. "Come on, girl. Take a breath."

The calf sneezed. Enzo's eyes went wide and he looked up at her. "Keep doing what you're doing. We're getting there." There was another sneeze and then a gasp for air. His large hands went still but stayed on the fragile body.

Momma was on her feet and nosing at her baby. Resa rolled back on her heels and rose. Enzo did the same, giving the mom room to check out her baby. He stood next to Resa and took her hand in his, entwining their fingers. "We did it." His voice was low and gravelly. "She's breathing."

"Yes, she is. It's pretty amazing, isn't it?"

The calf lifted her head. They moved back to the railing but stayed in the stall area. Enzo had dropped her hand but remained close. Resa shivered, but not from the cold.

Enzo left and came back with a red-and-black-plaid blanket that he dropped over her shoulders. "It's getting cold." There was no way she was going to explain that it hadn't been the temperature, but his nearness that had her reacting.

Leaving again, he was back quickly with their coffee cups. He must have refreshed them, because it was warm. Taking a deep breath, she pulled the rich aroma into her body. Had he always been this attentive and she just hadn't seen it, or was this a new side of him?

On his knees, he leaned back and balanced on his heels with one hand braced on his thigh. Sipping his coffee, his intense gaze stayed on the new baby.

The calf pushed up on her back legs but fell. She tried the front, but collapsed and just lay there, breathing heavily. The heifer nosed her.

"She's not in the clear yet, is she? How long does she have to be up and feeding?"

"Two hours. If she hasn't been able to nurse on her own within two hours, we'll have to intervene. It's critical we make sure she gets that first shot of antibody exposure from the colostrum."

After a long minute, the little calf tried again, until all four legs were supporting her. She was a bit on the wobbly side, but she flicked her tail.

Taking a step, she fell but didn't stay down long. Her mom nosed her and then ran her tongue over her head and back. Of course, that knocked her down again. But it didn't discourage her.

He laughed. "I find myself holding my breath. We have…" He flipped his wrist to study his watch. "An hour and forty-five more minutes before we can celebrate a successful birth. I can't even imagine how new parents must feel holding their baby for the first time. Watching them go off into the world. How did our parents do it without losing it?"

"I know, right? The cycle of life is messy and heartbreaking, but mostly beautiful. When I have the honor of watching new life enter the world, I'm amazed all over again at the glory of God."

She yawned. The day had suddenly caught up with her, and no amount of coffee was going to change that.

"Let me take you back to the house. You have work in the morning. I can finish this."

"Oh no, I'm used to working and waiting all hours. It's a rare baby born during office hours. It's still early. This isn't bad at all. I'm good, and I don't want to miss the last step."

They fell into silence as they watched the persistent calf getting to her feet and attempting to walk. Enzo refreshed their coffee. About another thirty minutes in, they had success.

The calf stayed on her feet and made it to her mother to feed. The heifer stood patiently, turning to watch the little one.

"They did it." She threw her arms around Enzo in a victory hug.

He grinned at her. "That was wondrous, and you get to do this with people?"

"I do. When things go well, it's absolutely life-affirming." Watching the newborn struggle and then make it to her mom filled Resa with such joy. The baby flicked her tail and almost fell over. "By afternoon tomorrow, she'll be running around bothering all the grown-ups. That's the disadvantage of being the first born. No playmates."

"Maybe that why us firstborns have the reputation of being too serious and bossy."

She laughed. "Could be. You and my sister Margarita have a lot of the same annoying habits in common."

"Margarita is a remarkable woman, so I'll take that as a compliment."

They took the supplies back to the office, cleaned what needed cleaning, replaced other items, and reshelved everything. They stopped at the railing and watched the calf and heifer for a few minutes before going to the horses.

Enzo must have checked on the horses at one point. They were now standing in a stall with access to hay and water. The leather bridles had been hooked over the gates.

She rubbed Sassy's muzzle and slipped the bit in. "You've been a good girl. There's an extra alfalfa square for you when we get to the stables."

"Tighten your cinch. I came and loosened them when I realized we were going to be here for a while."

She felt bad that she had been so focused on the cow and calf she had forgotten the comfort of the horses. "Thank you. I'm a bad horse mom."

"We all need backup now and then. You were busy. Thank you for coming out and taking care of this."

"You could have handled it."

"Thankfully, we'll never know if there could have been a different outcome if I'd been alone. Plus, I found it much better to work through this with someone very competent in the whole birthing thing. It's way out of my wheelhouse."

The horse bridled and ready, Resa put her boot in the stirrup and lifted herself into the saddle, waiting for Enzo. He stroked Lone Star's neck as he said something low. The gelding's ear flicked back and forth, listening.

With an ease of movement, like he had never left ranch life, he swung his body up into the saddle and settled in the seat in one fluid motion. He looked like he belonged there.

"Are you sure you want to go back to Colorado?"

At first, he didn't respond. Maybe he hadn't heard her, which might be for the best. The last thing she wanted was for him to think she was looking for a more personal relationship.

He sighed and moved his horse forward. "This last year has made me doubt my life choices."

Her heart rate doubled. What was he saying?

"But the faster everything is settled here, the faster I can get back to Colorado. That'll be better for everyone." He clicked to his horse and left the barn, heading out into the darkness. She nudged Sassy to follow.

The moon was bright and, in the east, the last rays of the sun slipped to the other side of the world. Even with the lunar light, it would take concentration to make sure they got back to the stables without mishap.

Why did she have to fall for the guys who were never going to give her the family she wanted?

Her body went tight. Oh no. She was in love with Enzo Flores.

*What was wrong with her?*

Enzo had been clear that his life was not here, and he was leaving as soon as he could. Why didn't she believe it when men told her they didn't want a family with her?

Her heart was being illogical again, and this would only lead to heartache. As long as he was in town, she wouldn't be dating anyone. All the men would be compared to Enzo, and it wasn't fair to them. Hopefully once he left, he would be out of sight and out of her head.

When had she lost her heart to her playground nemesis?

# Chapter Fourteen

Enzo had let his dad's gelding take the lead across the pasture and bring them home through the darkness. As light from the stables welcomed them back, he pulled up on the reins to let his eyes adjust to the new light. In more ways than one. Tonight, he'd experienced God in a way he had never expected, and it was overwhelming. Topped with his connection to Resa, he was reeling.

The knot in Enzo's stomach was back. He couldn't recall the last time he'd had such a deep and authentic conversation with anyone.

He had almost told her about Ryan and his fear that he had made some unknown mistake that had put the rookie in the line of fire. He never talked about his fears and doubts to anyone. Not his family, the counselors, or even his wife.

God was urging him to do something he wasn't comfortable doing. Sharing his fear and failures with Resa went against his survival instincts.

Resa and Sassy came up next to them. She dismounted. "You okay?"

In so many ways, he wasn't, but he also felt he was on the edge of a huge life-altering event if he trusted God. Could he? "I'm not sure. Tonight was something else."

She nodded, waiting for him to continue.

How did he even begin to explain this anger at himself for wasting so much time at being mad at God for the condition of the world when it was all about free will?

"I felt the love that God has for the world and realized we are the problem. We don't deserve that love."

"But He gives it to us anyway. It's pretty amazing. Witnessing the creation of life can stir up all sorts of feelings."

"Yeah." That's what all this was about. Watching the calf take her first breath… He swung his leg over, dismounted, and made his way to the post to tie his horse by the tack room.

They unsaddled and groomed their horses in silence. Resa took her tack in and came out with two buckets of feed and a smile. "I promised alfalfa cubes."

It was like candy to horses. Laying her hand flat, she gave one to Sassy. Then she handed him the other, along with a bucket. They went in separate directions as they led their horses to their stalls.

What about Resa? They had been in and out of each other's lives, yet he couldn't be the one to give her the life she wanted because he'd chosen another path. Because of his free will, she wasn't going to get the desire of her heart. That wasn't fair.

And that was exactly why he hated this type of discussion and reflection. Free will versus God's plan. Who won in that kind of situation?

The idea of self-determination, and what it meant to the world, bounced around in his head. He had become so focused on the bad in the world, he had turned his back on the cornerstone of everything his parents believed. It was easy to blame God for all the wrong in the world.

He had his hand against the warmth of Lone Star's neck and watched him eat.

The faith he'd grown up with had slipped away. God hadn't turned His back on Enzo or humanity. He was there waiting for them to turn to Him. One relationship at a time.

He sighed. He needed to remember that. Ana had asked him to take Lorenzo to church, and he told her he would. He had never lied to his sister before. In his head, he'd made excuses that he was bonding with Lorenzo. So much time and energy went into avoiding God.

There was a social on Wednesday night and a kids club for Lorenzo. He'd go. No excuses. That would be a good place to start. Ana would be home on Thursday.

Getting right with God would, he hoped, put the rest of his life on track. What better place than the church he'd grown up in and first believed?

Enzo caressed the horse's neck and shoulder. The muscles under the skin were sleek and strong. He used to feel that way. Now he just didn't know, and he hated the uncertainty.

A noise from the unsecured door brought him back to the present. He spun around, ready for an attack. Resa stood alone in the doorway. Long, graceful fingers were clasped in front of her. She glanced down, as if something had caught her attention on the ground, then she raised her chin and they made eye contact. Her mouth opened as if to say something, but she closed it again.

The light from the corridor surrounded her like a halo. How had he missed seeing her all these years? She was captivating.

"Hey." Her voice was low and raspy. "What has you so deep in thought?"

Wanting to be closer, he moved away from the horse but stopped halfway to her. Distance was good. "You."

Her eyes went wide and one hand went to her chest. "Me?"

"I wanted to thank you."

"Oh." She tilted her head. "But you did."

"No. Not for just coming to my rescue with the heifer. For the conversation. For talking with me and listening." He paused. The words needed to be edited before he spoke them; there was so much he wanted to tell her. But he had to keep a distance, for her sake. "A lot of…" His mouth went dry. He cleared his throat. "I had a lot of events this year that unsettled me. The kind that knock you off your feet and make you reevaluate everything. You know?"

She nodded in understanding. It was more than just a friendly, agreeable gesture. He could see that she genuinely empathized. He took a deep breath and one step closer to her. "The failure of my marriage was pretty much all my fault. And it happened way before I told my family. Tonight, I realized that I have always referred to my wife and my family as two separate groups. They shouldn't be. Brit accused me of not letting her in, and she was right."

"I doubt it was all your fault. Just like my relationship with Darren. We both did things that were wrong. We both hung on to the relationship for different reasons and were not willing to really deal with the problems. Relationships take two people working with God. Like a triangle. There has to be a life goal in common, and if you don't talk about it, or take God out of the equation, it falls apart."

She shrugged. "Playing the blame game doesn't help anyone. I…" She looked up at the loft above them before bringing her eyes back to him. "Our conversation tonight really helped clarify some things for me. Thank you for listening and for your insight." She smiled. "But I'll deny that last part if you tell anyone."

He chuckled. "Duly noted." He searched the depths of her dark eyes for answers to the questions he didn't even know. He took a step closer. "Resa."

"Yes?" She sounded a little breathless.

"You're going to be okay whatever you decide to do. You're going to be better than okay."

She nodded and looked down. Was she about to cry? Had he said the wrong thing?

He took another step toward her and held out his hand. Lone Star nudged him without warning and knocked him forward. Surprised, Resa jumped back and bumped into the wall. The halter hanging precariously on the edge of the hook fell. Instinctively, he lunged forward and caught it with his left hand. His right hand landed on her waist to balance her.

They both froze. She was literally in his arms. Part of his brain was yelling. *Back up! Space, man. Space.*

The other urged him closer. *This is what we've wanted for days. Go for it!* He understood the reason people talked about moths being drawn to a flame that would burn them. Call him Moth. The beautiful life-giving flame of hope was dangerously in his arms.

He should move. She hadn't fallen. He slipped the leather halter back onto the hook and stood there. Not shrinking from his touch, she blinked up at him with big eyes. His free hand came to rest lightly on the other side of her waist.

If she were smart, she'd step back, because he didn't think he was strong enough to pull away. They stood there, staring at each other. The warmth and confidence of who she was in this world radiated from her, pulling him in closer.

He waited two more heartbeats for her to back away from him, to step out of his touch, but she didn't. She stayed. Her big, cat eyes stared up at him, and everything in his world knew that this was right. Resa was the answer to all his questions.

She was a soft place in a harsh world. She was love; the kind humanity needed to stay human. She represented everything he fought to protect.

He leaned closer until the gentle feel of her breath subdued him. Surrounded by the comforting scent of jasmine and rich earth, he wanted to stay there forever. The distance between them completely disappeared.

His lips were welcomed with the softest pressure of hers; a softness that tasted of sweet oranges and a hint of cherry. He deepened the kiss, and her hands were on the back of his neck. A strong connection grounded him in her arms. Every thought, doubt and fear faded, leaving her and this kiss to fill his mind and spirit.

He was pushed from the side, forcing him to break contact with Resa.

*No.*

Lone Star nudged him again. He wanted his forelock rubbed.

For a moment, Enzo felt disjointed. Puffs of air came from his lungs in a haphazard manner. Obeying the command to scratch between the gelding's ears, he kept his head down. There was no way he'd survive eye contact with Resa. That kiss had turned his world upside down. Everything he knew to be true was false.

She moved to stand on the other side of the gelding. Putting the horse between them was a good move. Her laugh sounded forced. "I think someone wants your attention."

The horse had it. All of his attention stayed on his father's gelding. Lone Star was his touchstone to reality. He rubbed the horse's forelock. Mouth dry, Enzo licked his lips. It didn't help. His brain had dried up too. Not a single word that would be appropriate came to mind.

"I think he misses your dad." She had one hand on the top of the horse's neck and the other rubbed his muzzle.

Yeah, Enzo missed him too. The man was larger than life and took care of the people he loved. The land and animals too. Growing up, there was nothing his dad couldn't do. His dad hadn't stepped foot on the ranch until he'd dated the rancher's only child, Enzo's mom.

But there was no evidence of that by the time Enzo was old enough to follow after his dad. It was as if the dirt was in his blood. His father had had a purpose, found his path and fulfilled it. Enzo had thought he was on the right path, but there had been potholes lately.

Enzo had always been intimidated by his dad. His own dreams had been far away. "My dad is the best steward of the gifts he was given. I don't know anyone who takes care of the people in his life more. Even his horses."

His dad would be disappointed in Enzo's actions. He had just crossed a line with Resa that he should have never even been close to. "I always wanted to be more like him, and I'm not anywhere close."

"What? You save people for a living. That's, like, your job."

"No. I chase bad guys who have already hurt or are hurting people. Sometimes, I put my own people in the line of fire. My dad protects the people he loves. He builds up lives. As we speak, he's building an orphanage in Peru."

"And you're here making sure your sister and nephew are safe. Don't sell yourself short. You are a man to be admired too."

Did she see him like that? She wouldn't if she knew the truth.

Enzo closed his mouth, not sure what to say that wouldn't make this worse. The middle-school boy in his brain came out of hibernation, and was jumping around like a wild man, cheering and fist-bumping. But he knew this was bad. It was a mistake that would have consequences. He'd had no right to kiss Resa if he wasn't staying. His father would have his hide for this.

Gently, he backed Lone Star into the stall and waited for Resa to step out before he closed the gate. The horse tossed his head. "I'll be back tomorrow," he promised.

Taking a breath, he finally turned to her. "I'm sorry. That shouldn't have happened. It's been an eventful day and I…" He shook his head. "There's no excuse for my poor behavior. I'm sorry." That was weak. He'd already said that.

"Why, Mr. Flores…" With an exaggerated drawl, she batted her eyes and covered her heart with her hands. "Are you sayin' your intentions aren't pure? I thought this meant we were to be wed."

He rolled his eyes. "You're still a brat."

"I'm also a grown woman." Her voice was back at its normal pitch. "If I hadn't wanted you to kiss me, I would have walked out way before we touched." She put her hands on her hips. "I'm not going to faint. I get it. It didn't mean anything."

With that, she turned to leave. Her braid whipped around as she stomped out of the barn.

*Wait.* She had wanted him to kiss her before they'd gotten close? How long had she wanted to kiss him? And what had she meant when she'd said *it didn't mean anything*? He frowned. If she felt half of what he'd experienced, it most definitely meant *something*.

He went after her with some dignity. He didn't run. She was already halfway down the road and at the back door when he caught up with her. "Resa. We need to talk."

"I'm so sorry, Enzo." She stared at the house.

Taking his gaze off her, he turned to see what had upset her. The whole house was lit up. Several cars that had not been there before lined the front drive. It looked like a party. "What's happened?"

"The Espinozas."

"It's like your whole family is in the ranch house. Why?" His scowl deepened and he looked at his watch. It was eight thirty. Not as late as he'd thought, but still a little past the proper visiting hour.

He had a bad feeling about this. "Resa, do you have any idea what is going on?"

She shook her head and pulled her phone out of her back pocket. "No texts or calls." She looked up at him. "What if something happened to…" She ran to the back door.

He followed, praying that everyone he loved was safe.

# Chapter Fifteen

They both paused at the door and glanced at each other, then Enzo took hold of the door handle. Together, they would face whatever else the night wanted to bring. The smell of baking bread was the first thing Resa noticed. Then the aroma of deep cleaning.

The kitchen just about sparkled. Her mom walked out of the laundry room carrying a basket loaded with folded towels. Lorenzo was right behind her. A smaller basket balanced on his head.

"Tía Resa, Tío Enzo." He lowered the bundle and smiled. "I'm helping clean the house so grandma doesn't think we've been living like—"

"Lorenzo." Her mother's voice was sharp and cut him off smoothly.

"Oh. Sorry. I forgot it was a surprise."

Enzo dropped, balanced on his toes with his arms on his knees so he was eye to eye with his nephew.

"Grandma and Papa will be here in the morning."

Her mother clicked her tongue. "Well, the good thing is this boy can't lie."

His gaze shot to her mother. "My parents were able to leave Peru? When will they be here?"

"In the morning. Early." Yolanda sighed. "She called me so I can pick them up at the airport. The plan was to come in and surprise you. You know how she loves a dramatic entrance. This wasn't the plan, but God has His own. If we are smart, we change the path we thought we had laid out. He knows best for His people."

She waved to the activities going on past the kitchen. "I figured you've been so busy trying to keep everything together, you probably haven't had time to keep the house clean to the level she or Ana would expect. So me and the girls came over to help. How's the heifer and calf? You're back earlier than I expected," she asked as if she hadn't just turned everything in their world upside down.

Resa glanced at Enzo. He had that shell-shocked look she'd seen on many non-family members when her mother was on a mission.

"We were successful," she told her mom. "The heifer was able to do most of the work. It was just slow. But it's a little girl, and she was on her feet nursing when we left."

"Oh Enzo, your sister and parents will be pleased." She set the basket down. *"Bien hecho. Hacéis muy buena pareja."*

*"Momi,* we are not a couple."

Her mother waved her off. "You know what I mean. Good teamwork. Don't get so uptight. Y'all haven't eaten. Let me warm up the plates I have for you. Lorenzo, take your towels to the hallway bathroom."

"Yes, ma'am. Can I stay home from school tomorrow?"

"No. No," her mother answered. "Your grandparents want to pick you up from school after they speak to your *tío* and check out the ranch. Remember, it was supposed to be a surprise. Now, take the towels. ¡*Andale!* Josefina should have the bathroom all clean." Her mother moved to the refrigerator.

Through the wide archway between the kitchen and family room, Resa saw Margarita sweeping and her nieces and nephews dusting everything like an army of ants. Josefina was heading up the stairs with a caddy.

She dared another glance at Enzo. He hadn't moved. Her mother was making her nervous. She only fell into Spanish when she was excited, sad, or plotting something. Going to her mother's side, Resa took the foil squares from the plates and folded them. "*Momi*. What are you up to?"

"*¿Yo? ¿Por qué?*" Her mom looked all innocent.

"Because you only use so much Spanish when you are up to something."

"No. I'm just excited to see my old friend. Ana will be coming home soon. A new baby will be here. One that you will help bring into the world. Just like you helped Enzo tonight. He needed someone, and he called you because he trusts you. You work good together. There is just a lot going on, and I want the house to be in top shape for the homecoming and the new baby. We do this all the time for new moms."

Resa narrowed her eyes at her mother, trying to see past the explanation. It was true. This was a frequent practice of her mother and sisters, but not usually so late at night.

Her mother turned. "Sit, Enzo. You, too, Resa. You have worked hard today. Dinner will be ready soon. Do you want tea, milk or a soda to drink?" She stretched up to get two glasses.

Enzo was next to her. "I can get that."

"No. You will wash up and then sit." Her mother was small, but whether it was raising seven children on her own or being a preschool teacher, she issued commands just as expertly as any well-trained general.

Enzo sat and Resa joined him. "No point in trying to stop her now," she whispered.

One corner of his mouth quirked. "I'd love a Dr Pepper. After all that coffee, there's no point in cutting off the caffeine now."

Two ice-cold Dr Peppers and warm tortillas were placed in front of them. "I can't believe my parents will be here in the morning. Ana will be home soon if things go well." He didn't look as happy as she thought he would be at the news.

Did he want to stay? No. He was just worried. She needed to remember that he would be leaving soon.

She made sure to smile at him. "You've been successful at keeping the ranch working on schedule, and you safely delivered a calf tonight. You've done well."

"It was a rough start. I couldn't have done it without you." For a moment, they just stared at each other.

Resa tried not to glance at his lips, but it was hard. The kiss they had shared not that long ago seemed to be in another lifetime. In her gut, she knew it would stay with her forever. Nothing had ever felt more right than Enzo Flores's kiss. But he thought it was a mistake. Kissing her had been a mistake. All these feelings had to be buried now and never allowed to resurface.

"Resa." His voice was low. The one word sounded like it cut the tender skin of his mouth on its way out.

She took a deep breath and waited. Was he experiencing any of the responses and intensity that were burning in her? Even a fragment?

"*¡Aquí está!* Eat up!" Her mother's command brought her back from the edge of losing control of her emotions. She waved at their plates. "I will be in the bedrooms putting new sheets on, if you need me." She grabbed the basket and was gone.

At first, both of them just stared at the *carne asada*. He was the first to lift his face and look at her. "Your mother is something else."

"Yes. She is, and my two other sisters are right with her. They are up to something." She looked over his shoulder and found Margarita watching them. Her oldest sister smiled and then put her head down and pretended to be sweeping an area she had already swept.

"Up to something? You make it sound bad." He shot a weary glance to the front part of the house. "I must admit, I'm incredibly grateful I only have one sister. I don't know if I would have survived a whole family of them." He lifted his tall glass and his Adam's apple moved up and down as he took a prolonged drink of his soda. Technically, she knew the bump was just part of the thyroid cartilage. Everyone had one.

Her gaze took in the detailed movement of his throat. How could such a normal part of the human body be so masculine? Never in her life had she wanted to lean over and...

Closing her eyes, she refocused. *Girl, look somewhere else.*

There was a soft thud. Blinking, she made sure to keep her gaze down on the table. His hands were still holding the soda. Condensation dripped through the long and capable fingers wrapped around the glass.

She'd seen those hands fix the tiniest part of an irrigation system, move heavy bags of feed and rub life into the heart of a newborn calf. Now she was afraid they held her heart.

Enzo twisted around and then dug into his meal with a sigh. For a moment, he closed his eyes and might have moaned. Her mother's cooking had that effect on people.

"Whatever she's up to, if she keeps feeding me, I'm sure I'll go along without argument."

She snorted. "That's how she gets you. But I'm not sure it'll work this time." Her mother's will was not strong enough to change Enzo's life plans.

With another bite, he looked at her, a question in his eyes.

"She thinks we make a great couple, and I'm sure she's plotting our wedding within the next year."

He coughed.

Resa tilted her head and pressed her lips together so as not to react.

He dropped his fork, horror stamped on his face instead of food-induced bliss.

"What? It doesn't taste as good now? No longer following my mother blindly into whatever scheme she is laying out?" His rejection was a little too fast for her ego not to take a hit. Humor was always a safe way to hide any hurt.

If he knew that she had fallen in love with him, he'd panic. She frowned. He'd probably blame her, but it wasn't like she'd set out to do this. She knew better, but her mother didn't.

One look at the right time and her mother had probably known Resa was in love before she'd realized it herself.

Pushing the beef around on her plate, she was afraid to make eye contact with him. What if he saw the truth? She'd be mortified. "That's what all the Spanish and plotting was about. My mother is a hopeless romantic. Her mission in life is to make sure all her children are happily married. She's way too optimistic for this world of heartbreak."

With what she hoped was a sweet smile, Resa dared to look up at him, but he was staring at his plate.

She couldn't take the silence. "I don't know how much you remember about my parents. They were so in love. My childhood memories are full of dancing and singing in the kitchen. Joy and laughter were part of small moments and big events. Even when we thought my little brother was lost and most likely dead, they clung to each other and their faith. Then cancer came in and took my father before any of us had time to process that he was sick. Through it all, they loved each other and loved us."

Her mother had hardly missed a step. Now, as an adult, Resa realized there had to have been a lot of lonely nights where her mother cried herself to sleep. But never in front of her children. Her faith had carried them all through.

"She wants that deep connection for each of us. This life is tragically beautiful. Her hope and faith is awe-inspiring. But I think I'm coming to realize not all of us get that in our life. At least, not when we think we should get it." There was no way she'd be able to move quickly from these feelings she had for Enzo.

He would leave, and she would continue with her life and fulfill her purpose. That would fill her heart. It had to.

He picked up his fork and stared at it. "I love well-made fountain pens."

"Okay. That's random."

The corner of his mouth lifted in the most beautiful half grin. Whenever she managed to get that relaxed expression from him, she counted it a win.

"Listen. I do my best thinking by writing notes and making connections. My mom knows this about me and, a couple of years ago, she gave me a StarWalker by Montblanc. I use it every day. She had Proverbs 14:13 engraved on it. It's a strange verse for her to give me. One she knew I would see every day. It didn't make any sense. When I asked her about it, she said I would understand when I needed to." He chuckled. "I think I just got it." He took a bite.

"What? You're not going to tell me the verse? Proverbs is big—14:13 is not ringing any bells. I know you've memorized it. Spit it out."

"You have no patience." He took another bite and winked at her.

"Not with you. Now you're toying with me."

Setting down his fork, he leaned back. "'Even in laughter the heart is sorrowful, and the end of that mirth is heaviness.'"

She frowned. "You're right. That's a weird one for her to put on your pen." She strolled through the words again. "You deal with a lot of heaviness with your work. Is she warning you not to live in the heaviness and darkness?"

"That could be. But I don't think it's meant to tell me what to do or not do. It's a bit of truth about life. She wants me to remember that laughter and heartache, joy and grief, are a part of life. God is there through it all. We can't control the people around us, but we can enjoy the joy and accept the grief. It's the cycle of life, and you can't have one without the other."

"Wow. That's deep. It just came to you?" She leaned forward.

"Not really. I mean, it all came together, but she planted the verse two years ago. This time at the ranch with you has brought so many things into focus. I wasn't in a good place when I got here. My last mission didn't go as planned."

"I'm sorry. I know how important what you do at the FBI is to you." Clenching her fist under the table, she kept herself from reaching out to him. Had innocent people been hurt? Had he lost a team member? Worse-case scenarios bounced in her head. She held back, giving him space to say more. Would he? He never shared weaknesses.

His chest expanded with the deep breath of air. "There was a miscalculation. Something went wrong and one of my guys, a rookie, was injured."

That bump in his throat went up and down. The urge to hug him was getting hard to push down, but she didn't want to scare him, so she waited again.

"He's in a coma." Another long pause. "I'm on leave while an investigation is being done. I don't know if he is going to heal, be disabled for life, or even if he'll live."

His head dropped. When he finally raised his chin, he avoided her and looked out the dark window. "*I* was the lead. I was responsible for connecting all the information gathered from various sources. My job was to analyze the risks and reactions and then lay out a plan for each. Everything was in place, but something went wrong. The events keep running through my head step by step. I've gone over each minute in slow motion, trying to find the mistake I made."

"But you're working with a criminal element in an unsecured environment. You can't control everything. Do they expect you to?"

"When I put people in the line of fire, I expect that I've created the best plan with the best outcome."

"Has anyone ever been hurt on a mission you've lead?"

"No. I have a clean record. Until now. And Ryan is paying for my mistake."

"But you don't know for sure it was your mistake. That's why there's an investigation." Not able to stop herself from comforting him, she took his hand into hers. "Let them do their job. When do you expect to hear from them?"

"I called Friday to check on Ryan. No news." He turned his hand over and wrapped his fingers around hers. "Thank you."

"It's hard to carry that kind of burden alone. You don't have to." She leaned closer. The need to tell him she loved him boiled and threatened to overflow. But it could totally backfire and put them in a worse place than where they'd started.

Enzo needed a place of rest and calm. Hearing that she loved him would upset that cart in one motion. She shifted so there was more space between them, but he still held her hand. She would have to be happy with this for now. Maybe tomorrow she would be brave enough to tell him how she felt.

# Chapter Sixteen

Enzo spent the late morning and early afternoon riding with his parents. He rode between them as they made their way back to the stables. His dad was impressed with the improvements his sister had made on the ranch.

"Son, you've stepped in and picked up the reins as if you were paying attention back when you were in school." His father chuckled at his own joke.

"Don't start in on him. We just got home," his mother said as she rode Sassy. "You're going to be able to stay awhile, right? I hope you don't have to rush back."

There was a part of him that wanted to stay forever, but that was just emotions clouding his judgment. "I'm expecting a call soon. Then I'll know what my next move is"

"Your next move? Are you thinking about leaving the FBI?" His father's voice was rough.

"Not necessarily. But I would like to get back to Texas and be closer to the ranch."

His mother gasped. "They have headquarters in Houston. That is so close. It can be a day trip."

He grinned. "I know, Mom. But I haven't said anything because I'm not sure, and it depends on several other moves outside of my control. There is also a promotion that would take me back to Washington."

"No." She sounded devastated.

He closed his eyes. "There is a lot going on. I really shouldn't have said anything. Now you're upset."

They approached the barn. "Of course, I'm upset. But I'll be upset when you drive back to Colorado. So there is that. It's been a long time, and I just want you home."

"Really? You're the one living in Peru." He grinned at her as he dismounted. He walked over to Sassy and held her reins as he used his other hand to help his mom get out of the saddle. Growing up, she had been a trick rider, and seeing her move slowly to the ground reminded him that his parents were aging. Living in another state, it was easy to forget.

"Goodness me." She was out of breath. "It's been a while since I've spent this much time on a horse." Turning, she stood in front of him and cupped his face like she had when he was younger and she wanted to make sure he was listening. "You do good work in the world, but I'm worried about you. When you first got married, I thought she would help ground you, but you became even more distant. Then the divorce."

"I'm sorry, Mom. I know I disappointed you."

"No." She tapped his face. "Listen to me. I'm worried about your heart and your relationship with God. That she left didn't surprise me. She never even tried to be part of our family."

He pulled back, ashamed that he had allowed his marriage to fail. "That was my fault. I never brought her home."

"But I called. Ana called." One hand on her hip, his mother waved the other. "We tried to connect with her. I knew you traveled, so we invited her to come down while you were out of town. We hinted that we would love to visit, but she never invited us. How can you build a family with someone who doesn't want to be a part *of* your family? I was worried."

"You never said anything. I didn't know you had called."

"*¿De verdad?*" His dad was offended for his wife. He only broke out the Spanish when he was upset. "She never told you that your mom reached out to her?"

"No." He looked at his mother. "Why didn't you tell me?"

"I didn't know what was going on in your marriage, and if you didn't want to talk to me about it, it was none of my business." There was moisture in her eyes, but she didn't cry. "I waited for you to talk to me, but you never did. You've always been hard to read and closed off. I wasn't sure how to help. I didn't want to make it worse. You have a dark, stressful job. How long was she gone before you told us?" She crossed her arms and raised one brow, head tilted.

"She left about a year ago."

His mother softened. "Oh, *mijo*."

His dad came around and put his hand on Enzo's shoulder. "Son, you should have come to us. Dealing with this alone isn't good for your heart or head."

"*Popi*, no one in our family is divorced. I knew you'd be upset about it."

His mother had one hand back on his face. "I'm upset because your heart was hurt. You come from a long line of prayer warriors. It doesn't make marriage or life any easier, but when it gets too hard to handle, we turn to God. It's that common faith that helps us stay together. Was she a believer?"

"Not really. Not like you."

"Were you going to church or at least reading your Bible? I sent you devotionals." The tilt of her chin and look in her eye indicated that she already knew the answer.

Guilt clogged his throat, so he just shook his head.

"Oh, baby. This world is a big ugly mess. We can't handle it alone. Our strength comes from God. That's how we've stayed together. God is the needle we both use to navigate. But that is all behind us." She rubbed her hands and threw them in the air as if getting rid of the bad vibes. "It's a new start. Move forward with God."

"I'm hungry." His father grumbled and then led Lone Star to the crosstie. "Let's put the horses up and get something to eat."

They each took care of their horses and turned them out in the small pasture. Together, they walked to the back porch.

His father placed a hand on his shoulder. "I'm pleased with the condition of the ranch. Everything is in better shape than when we left. Your sister has done a spectacular job. Don't tell her this, but I was wrong about some of the ideas I shot down a few years ago. You've done well stepping in for her. Children should be better than their parents, and you both make me proud. It could be good timing if you were ready to move home and run the ranch with your sister."

"I can't take too much credit. Resa has helped me every step of the way. I'm pretty sure you would have found a huge mess if she had not been here."

"Yes. I've heard everything about you and Resa. Another reason you should be moving home." There was so much hope in his mother's voice.

"Mom, we just finished talking about my failed marriage. Resa wants kids and the whole thing. I'm not that man."

"Why not? Brittany was not the one you were meant to be with. When two people fit, it's a beautiful thing. I hear you make a wonderful team. You both helped little Lorenzo through this hard time, and you delivered calves without any problems. Sounds like a perfect match to me. Now *she* is someone I can see fitting right into our family. She practically lived here growing up. I couldn't think of a better wife for you if you asked me to pick."

"I didn't ask. It was one calf, and Lorenzo hated me when I first got here because he only wanted his dad. Resa fixed it. I was clueless." Opening the screen door, he let his mother in and then his father.

"Sorry, son. I told her not to get her hopes up, but she wants to see you happy."

He followed his parents inside.

"Resa!" His mother's joyful greeting warned him, but it was still a twist to his heart to see her in the kitchen with his mother hugging her. How did Resa make this old house feel like home in a way it never had in his childhood?

"I'm so excited you're here. We were just talking about you," his mom said.

Over his mother's shoulder, Resa sent him a questioning look. He just mouthed the word *mothers* and gave her a fake smile.

Resa laughed. She stepped back and looked at his mom. "One of my patients lives on the Wilson ranch, and I had a home visit with her. On my way back, I thought I would stop by to see you. After riding all morning, I figured you'd be hungry, and you must be tired after all the travel to get home." She gave his father a hug and waved them to the table. "I made lunch if you want some."

"Oh, what a delight you are. Enzo was telling us how you came in and saved him. You make the perfect team."

"Mom, that's not what I said." He leaned on the counter and crossed his arms. "I was telling them how much I appreciated all your help. Apparently, our mothers have been talking and plotting."

His mother laughed. "You make it sound like something bad. All we want is for our babies to be happy, and if you make each other happy... Well, then, what could be better? You both know each other so well. It's perfect."

"Mrs. Flores, I believe Enzo plans to go back to Colorado as soon as...things are settled here." She shot him an apologetic smile and then turned back to the stove.

She was flipping toasted bread. Was she making grilled cheese sandwiches? His stomach grumbled. He sneaked a peek at the pot on the stove. Tomato soup.

Did she know this was his favorite lunch? Even during the summer? His mother must have told her, and now they were all messing with him.

"Oh, did you hear he might be moving to the Houston office."

Resa's head jerked up in his direction with a confused expression. "Really? He didn't mention that. But then, why would he?" She flashed a stiff smile. With an oversized spatula, she slid the sandwich onto a plate. "I hope this is okay. I had a craving for grilled cheese and tomato soup."

Going back to the stove, she filled four giant

mugs with the rich red soup. He pushed the odd twinge of guilt away. There was not a single reason he should have told her. Not a single one.

"That's interesting. It's Enzo's favorite. Growing up, he would have been happy to have this every day. I'll get the tea."

"I'll get it, Mom. I'm already up." He gathered four glasses and then pulled the tea from the refrigerator.

Resa sat the mugs of soup on the table as Enzo turned to pour the tea into the glasses with ice. Their elbows bumped and they paused. He hadn't realized they were standing so close to each other.

"Sorry," he mumbled and stepped to the left.

"It's good." But she didn't lift her face and give him the smile he had started looking for each day.

"Oh, Resa. Your mother is right. The two of you are perfect together."

He sighed and moved to the opposite end of the table. "Mom, please don't make this awkward. We are not a couple. There is no *together*. She has been helping me out, and I'm grateful. But she's right. I'm leaving soon. Even if it's to Houston. That is still not Port Del Mar. Resa has moved home, and she knows what she wants. Her clients are here. This is where she is building her future. Please don't make this into more than what it is. We're friends."

Resa sat two seats away from him. "We're friends. The good news is that, in a few more days, it will be safe for Ana to deliver at home. How do we coordinate moving her back here?"

Good. She was changing the subject. He didn't think he could handle any more of his mother talking about them as a couple. In a perfect world, he would give anything to share a life with Resa, here or anywhere she was, but the world was far from perfect, and he was even farther.

If the news was bad from the FBI, would he move home? Even if he was in Port Del Mar, he wasn't sure he could give Resa what she wanted. She was light, and he was afraid of smothering that light. He hadn't been able to make Brit happy. What made him think Resa would survive marriage to him?

His phone vibrated in his pocket. Checking his watch, he saw his director's name. "This is the Bureau." He stood and pulled the phone out of his pocket. "I've got to take it."

"Of course." Resa's golden-brown eyes wished him good news as she gave him a slight nod.

His stomach was in knots. This was the call he'd been waiting for. He sent a prayer that

Ryan was awake and on the way to a full recovery. *Please God, give me peace, no matter the news.*

What if they'd found it was his mistake that had put the kid in the hospital? This was the call that would take him back to Colorado or send him on a new journey. His new faith was going to be tested. Was he ready?

Resa stirred her soup. That had to be the call he'd been waiting for. She bowed her head for a moment and prayed Enzo would feel God's peace regardless of the news. She knew he was too hard on himself.

A gentle nudge brought her back to the people she shared the table with. "He's been waiting for a call. I pray he hears good news, and if not, that he has peace about him."

"That's a wonderful prayer." His sweet mother lowered her head and Mr. Flores joined her.

After a moment of silence, Enzo's father spoke. "Dear God, we lift our son up to You just like we did the day he was born. We pray he opens his heart to You, and he follows the path You have for him. I pray over us here at the table that we have acceptance of whatever You have for him. Even if it is not what we wish for. In Jesus's name we pray. Amen."

"Amen," Resa echoed Mr. Flores.

"I have to admit…" Enzo's mother took Resa's hand in hers. "I want him home, and I would love to see you together, but my dear husband is right. We find joy when we follow God's wishes."

Resa nodded. "Y'all are going into town to pick up Lorenzo?"

"Yes. I'm going to take a shower and maybe a quick nap," Mr. Flores said and left the kitchen.

"I'm so excited to see Lorenzo. I'm sure he has grown a foot. We will be driving over to the hospital to visit Ana. Is there anything you need us to pick up for you?"

"No. I'll clean up here and then head back to town. I have a few late-afternoon appointments." Resa stood and gathered the plates.

Mrs. Flores came up next to her and put an arm around her shoulders. "In my mind, I see the two of you together. Your mother says you love him."

"My mother says a great deal of things."

"And most of them are true. If this is, don't give up on him. The world has surrounded him in darkness, and I think he lost his way, but he's coming back. I see it in his eyes. As a child, I couldn't tell what he was thinking, but I can see he cares for you, and in his mind, that can be dangerous."

"I know. But if he can't be open with himself, how can we even build a relationship?" She laid her head against the side of Enzo and Ana's mother. This woman had been a guiding light in her childhood. "Even if I do admit I love him, it might just scare him."

Standing straighter and patting Resa's hands, the older woman nodded. "I know. Just give him a little time. That's all I ask."

Resa really didn't have a choice. It wasn't like she was going to be falling in love with someone else while Enzo had her heart. She just didn't see him accepting that gift from her. All she knew was that she wanted a relationship with a partner who stood on equal ground with her. He didn't have to proclaim his undying devotion every day, but he had to at least learn to speak one of her love languages. Was it too much to ask for someone to value her enough to make sure she felt cherished and loved? She didn't want to settle for convenience.

She had spent too many years being the only one who gave. Was it wrong to want someone to chase after her?

# Chapter Seventeen

Out of habit, Resa went to the ranch house to have breakfast with Lorenzo. Even though Ana had returned home two days ago, and his grandparents were there, Resa still went. It was easier for everyone if she drove Lorenzo to school on her way into town. She also missed Enzo. A feeling she needed to get use to.

Was he trying to make a point by avoiding her? Or had they just been missing each other due to circumstances. Jazz and her husband had called. The mother of two, now three had gone into labor early last evening, and their new baby girl had entered the world at one in the morning.

She hadn't seen Enzo since he'd gotten the call from the FBI. She'd hoped he would reach out, come over to her place after his call, but he hadn't. Was his young agent still in a coma?

Had things gotten worse? Had he shut down and didn't want to talk? No one else knew what was going on in Colorado, so avoiding her would make sense. But it still hurt.

She walked into the kitchen and was greeted with lots of hollering and tears. "What's wrong?"

Ana was at the table crying. "It's Julian."

Resa's stomach fell and she gripped the back of the chair. She immediately sought out Enzo. He was holding his nephew, and they wore identical smiles. Huge, wide, teeth-flashing grins.

"Daddy's coming home! We're going to get him at the airport tonight!"

She covered her mouth. "Oh." Her own tears fell. Tears of relief. She rushed to Ana. "He's coming home today?"

Her friend nodded. "He wasn't allowed to say anything or contact us until he was back on American soil. He's flying into Houston. Mom and Dad are going to take Lorenzo to pick him up and bring him home. He'll be here tonight." She started crying again.

Putting her arm around her, she rubbed Ana's back. "It's okay. Just make sure to breathe." Together, they took a deep breath and let it out. Then, for no obvious reason, they giggled. Ana wiped at the tears on her face, but the giggles were uncontrollable.

"Mommy, are you okay?"

She nodded. "Yes. I'm just so happy we're going to see your daddy, and that you get to bring him home."

"I'm making pancakes and bacon," Mr. Flores announced. "Then we can pack for the road trip."

Resa glanced at the front door. "Looks like you are already packed."

"Those are Tío Enzo's. He's going back to Colorado."

She almost doubled over from the sharp pain in her middle. Her breath was nowhere to be found. Enzo was suddenly next to her, his hand on her arm. "I was coming over to your house when we got the call."

"You're leaving. Going back to your job with the FBI."

The joy in the room had vanished. There was a heavy silence. Mr. Flores cleared his throat. "He was at the back door when we got the news. I think his plan was to meet you and talk first."

"Thanks, Dad. Would you join me on the back porch, Resa?" His hand slipped down into hers and gently tugged at her to follow him. She pulled her hand from his grasp and went out the door. At the edge of the steps, she stopped and wrapped her arms around her middle.

Why was she acting so surprised? She'd known this was coming. The FBI was Enzo's life. He'd chosen it over his first wife, why would he make a different choice with her?

"Resa."

She walked away from him, crossing the drive to her front porch. It was cold and drizzling. The weather matched her mood. Her porch faced the east, and she wanted to see the sun rise. A new day meant new opportunities to help the women in her community.

"Resa. Please." Enzo's boots crunched the grave as he followed her.

Ignoring him, she sat on her rocker. There wasn't another place to sit. Perfect because he wouldn't be staying.

He stopped on her front step.

She kept her gaze on the wide horizon. "When they called, did you get an update on Ryan? I've been praying for him."

"Thank you. Yes. He came out of the coma, and he's in recovery. It looks promising, but it will be a long road for him."

"That's great. So the investigation was finalized?"

"Mostly. I need to complete some paperwork and we have a few new witnesses now that Ryan has filled in some holes. I need to do that in person."

"The mission failing wasn't because of anything you did or didn't do, was it?" This morning, there was no sunrise. The heavy gray clouds blanketed the sky.

"No. Ryan doesn't remember any of the shooting, but he told them everything leading up to it. He broke protocol. There was a group of young people, children really, who were about to be moved. We were not aware of that. Our informants just knew about the drug and weapon deals. No one had mentioned even a possibility of human trafficking. Ryan saw how young they were and, in a panic, he moved to stop it. He was afraid that if he called to update the information, it would be too late."

She nodded. "It came down to information you didn't have and his inexperience and good heart."

"Yeah." He put his hands in his pockets and looked to the horizon. The closed-off, hard-to-read Enzo was back. "I was going to tell you that night, but you were out late at the De La Rosa house. Congratulations on another successful delivery."

"Thank you. I know you were at the barns. I hear there are two new calves."

"We are up to four now. It's been busy. I really wasn't trying to avoid you."

"We both have phones. We both are used to weird hours. If you had wanted to talk to me, you would have."

He didn't reply.

The clouds were a moody gray and moved into surreal formations. Pop-up storms were a norm. She wondered if they would be around all day.

"I don't know what to say to you. You know I care about you, but I have to go back to my job. I've spent my whole life training for and building this career. There might be an opening in Houston later this year. I've talked to my director about moving back to Texas, but I won't ask you to move to Colorado. It wouldn't be fair."

She took her gaze off the building storm and studied him. "I love you, Enzo. But I don't think you're ready to be loved. I made a promise to myself that I wouldn't chase down a husband. I spent years chasing Darren. The sad part is, I didn't love him fully. Of course, I didn't realize that until I fell for you. Whatever is between us is stronger than anything I've ever experienced, but it can't be one-sided."

He turned to her, and with an intensity she had never seen in his eyes, he leaned in close.

"That's what scares me the most. I couldn't give Brit what she needed, and she was low maintenance. You scare me. I fear you'll expect things I'm not capable of giving. I'd never in a million years intentionally hurt you. But I can't promise that I won't hurt you by just being me. That would destroy me."

She pulled the quilt draped on the back of her rocking chair and laid it across her lap, snuggling into its warmth. It wasn't enough. It wasn't just the air that had dropped in temperature. Her heart had a new chill to it that wouldn't go away easily.

"I want to thank you for everything you've done for me and my family. It's…" He sighed. "I don't know if I'm coming back, so if you start dating again, I understand."

Her throat hurt. All she could manage was a jerky nod.

"I'm going to load my car, but I'll wait until tomorrow to leave since Julian's coming home tonight. I hope you'll be at dinner tonight. Please don't let me chase you away."

She pulled the quilt around her. "Let Ana know I'll come over around one to check on her. Make sure she doesn't start moving heavy furniture or doing any deep cleaning with the excitement of Julian coming home."

He nodded and then stood there for a little longer as if waiting for her to say or do something. She didn't. She had said her piece. If he wanted to be loved by her, he was going to have to ask.

Finally, he turned to leave, and she realized she had one question. "Enzo, why now? Ana is about to have the baby. Your parents just got back. Why leave now?"

"The FBI needs me. The ranch, my family, they don't. They're all good. They're going to be fine, better than fine now that Julian's back for good." He lowered his head and shuffled the tip of his boot in the red gravel. "I don't want you to start needing me. I know there's a connection between us, and I'm afraid the longer I stay, the more likely it will be that you'll get hurt. Leaving now is best for everyone."

She nodded as if that made any sense. She was sure it did to him. As brave as he was at facing the bad guys and protecting the country, he was a coward emotionally.

The urge to stand and yell at him was fierce. But her mom taught her to think about her words. Was it true? Yes. He was being a coward. Was it helpful? Maybe. If he would listen to her. That was unlikely. So no. Lastly, would it help the situation or change anything? No. He would remain the stubborn self-sacrificing hero, and she would be yelling for no reason other than to feel better.

She kept her mouth shut as he made his way across the driveway. Once he was out of sight the tears slid down her checks.

Enzo slammed the door and stood in the entryway. His last bag was in the Bronco, and he didn't have anything to do. As soon as he had come in from talking with Resa, his dad had grabbed him to go check out the heifers.

It was a good thing they'd taken their slickers. The small storm had turned into a gully washer. With the heifers secured in the barn, they'd headed for the house. His dad had tried to talk about Resa and the decision to return to the FBI, but Enzo hadn't been in the mood.

How could he have a conversation about something that he couldn't sort out himself? He knew he was walking away from the best woman he'd ever known, but he didn't know how to stop.

Restless, he went back out the door and moved to the front porch. He'd been standing right here when he had heard her the first night he was home.

Across the driveway, through the heavy sheets of rain, Resa's house looked empty. Her car was gone, so she must have gone to town. He looked at his watch. She said she'd be back at one.

His parents came into the living room with Lorenzo. The boy was still bouncing with the thought of his dad coming home. He looked at Enzo. "Can you stay, Tio Enzo? I'm going to miss you. So will Tia Resa. When you leave, she'll be sad. Do you have friends or a pet where you live?"

*No, he had coworkers.* Moving closer, he squeezed the small shoulder. "I think Resa would love being close to you." The thought of Resa being alone or sad ate at his gut. He was already hurting her.

"We're off," his dad said. "Thought it would be a good idea to leave early with this rain."

"Be careful. Text me at the midway point and when you get to the airport." He didn't like the idea of them going out in this without him, but they had all decided he would stay with Ana. In case of an emergency, he could get her to the hospital the fastest. Not that he or his father had told anyone else their plan.

He and his sister stood on the porch and waved as the car drove away.

"I can't believe I'll have Julian by my side tonight," Ana said and wrapped her sweater tighter around her. It was getting cold, and the last thing she needed was to get wet.

"Let's go inside. I'll make you some tea." They settled in the living room. She had opened one of the photo books their mother had ordered online. He hadn't seen them yet. This one was of Lorenzo's first three years of life, most of which Enzo had missed. Time was too precious to waste.

"I promise I'll come home more. At least once a quarter."

"We'll see. You always were looking out past our porch and past the city limits. We were too small for your big-world view."

He looked at her. "You find the smallness comforting?"

She shrugged. "It was where I was needed."

He frowned. "What do you mean? After high school, you went to the University of Houston for two years and then came home. You moved two hours away, and it was too far."

"That's not true. I loved being there. I loved my classes, and of course, that's where I met Julian, but then Grandpa had a bad fall. He couldn't do the work anymore, and Mom was worried about Dad. She asked me to come home. It wasn't a hard decision. I love the ranch, so I talked to Julian, and we moved back."

"No one told me what was going on."

"You were out of the country on a mission. But it's okay. You had bigger things to do, and our parents needed one of us to stay. Julian went into the reserves instead of joining the navy. We made a life. It's been good. Don't look so put out. We're all where we're supposed to be."

"Did you and Julian have other plans before they asked you to come back?"

She shrugged and took a sip of her tea. She closed her eyes for a minute and took some deep breaths.

"Ana. Are you okay? Do I need to call Resa?"

"No. Just taking the time to breathe. We had talked about going around the world as a military family. It sounded exciting, but my heart wasn't set on it. No crushed dreams in my life."

"But you didn't get to choose. Because everyone thought my goals were too important to interrupt? That wasn't fair to you or Julian."

"Enzo. We didn't do anything we didn't want to do. Have we done all the things we dreamed about? No. But that's life. We make choices. I'm happy where I am. I'll be happier once my husband is back in my arms." She grinned, and then a flash of pain crossed her face.

"I'm calling Resa." He pulled his phone out.

"It's the middle of the morning. She has appointments. Don't bother her. Now, if you want to call her to tell her you're an idiot, by all means, go for it."

"Why would I do that?"

"Because you're in love with her, but you're too much of a coward to admit it. Are you also lying to yourself?"

"I don't know how I feel." But he did. He loved her. He loved her in a way he'd never experienced before, which made him really sad for Brit. They hadn't had a chance.

"Well, big brother, let me spell it out for you. You love her, and it scares you because you like being in control. You can't control love. I have a theory that you have loved her since we were teenagers. That's why she scares you. All your neatly laid-out plans would have been blown to smithereens if you'd admitted you loved her. What would you have done if—" She yelled and doubled over.

He grabbed her hand. "That was less than three minutes from the last time I noticed you had a pain and tried to pretend you didn't. I've noticed four of them in less than ten minutes. How long have you been having contractions?"

"All morning, but then they go away for thirty minutes or so. I did this with Lorenzo and— Ohhh." She squeezed his hand. "It went on for hours. This is coming too fast."

Thunder rattled the house and a flash of

lightning followed. The kind that blinds you for a bit. The lights flickered.

"Do we have time to get you to the hospital?"

She doubled over and panted a few times. "Call Resa. You're not driving me anywhere."

More thunder and lightning proved the storm was getting stronger. He called Resa and hoped she hadn't blocked him.

"Enzo, everything okay?" It sounded like she was in her car.

"Ana's having contractions. They're running hard and fast. The last two have been a few minutes apart."

"I'm feeling better now," Ana said. "Are you on your way?"

"Yes. My last appointment was canceled, so I left the office early. I had a feeling between this storm rolling in and all the excitement over Julian, we might be meeting your baby girl today."

"Enzo will be very relieved when you get here. He was trying to play it cool, but now he's freaking out."

"I'm not freaking out. I just wish you had told me sooner. I would have called Resa sooner. I'm not trained for human delivery."

Resa dared to laugh at the other end of the phone. "Ana, are you comfortable, or do you want to go to your room?"

He hadn't even thought to ask her that. "I can carry her to her room." It would give him something to do.

"I can walk. Just give me your arm in case another contraction hits."

Resa stayed on the phone with them while he settled Ana in the bedroom. There was a list of items and steps to take in case of an emergency on the bedside table. He prayed he wouldn't have to use it. "How far out are you?"

"I'm at the entrance of the ranch. So, less than a minute away. You are both doing great. I'm going to disconnect now."

He held the phone like a safety vest, even though she was gone. The urge to pull her close and never let her go nearly brought him to his knees. A low, deadly growl came from his sister, interrupting his thoughts.

He'd deal with that later. Right now he had to make sure they all survived this day.

# Chapter Eighteen

Resa came in and reassured Enzo they were prepared and ready, then she sent him away with a list of items to gather. That should keep him busy while she examined Ana. Things were moving fast. *Thank you, God, for sending me home early.*

Enzo was a very capable man, but delivering his sister's baby might have been more than he could have handled if she had been thirty minutes later.

He sat on a chair at his sister's shoulder and held her hand. His gaze stayed glued to Ana's face as he encouraged her and allowed her to yell at him. Then she would smile and laugh at a story he told her.

"Should I call our parents? Julian should be arriving soon."

"No." Ana panted. "There's nothing they can

do but worry at this point." She gripped his arm and they counted. She blew out a large puff of air. "When she arrives, we'll call."

The storm whipped around them, streaking through the sky and throwing a fit to make any two-year-old proud.

He agreed with everything she'd said and that made her mad too. At one point, he dared to glance at Resa.

She nodded. "Everything looks great. It's not going to be much longer."

Shortly after, she was lifting the little girl and handing her to her mother.

He might have forgotten how to breathe.

Resa nudged him. "Air in. Air out. I have a little more work to do, so you're not allowed to pass out on me now. You made it through the worst of it."

He nodded. "You're amazing," he told his sister.

"Lorina, this is your *tío*, Enzo. He kept us safe during the storm." Ana looked up at him with a serene smile. "Do you want to hold her?"

There were tears in his eyes. "I shouldn't."

Ana nodded. "It's important for her to bond with the key people in her life. You're one of those people. You will be part of her life story."

Ana shifted the baby and placed the tiny bundle in his arms.

Enzo rocked back and forth. He didn't even know he was doing it.

"She's a miracle." He touched the tiny nose with his finger and looked at her hands. "Ana, I can't even put into words the…" Emotions were pouring from him.

"Love," Resa supplied. "It's an overpowering, all-consuming love. God gives it to us as a gift for the challenging times. And it helps us protect the most vulnerable."

He nodded. "It's all-consuming." He looked at his sister. "You did so good. Here." He gently placed the baby back Ana's arms. "You've worked hard today. I'm going to make dinner. Your choice."

"Lasagna." Her eyes lit up. "Remember when you had the world geography lesson in ninth grade. You had to bring an authentic dish from your assigned country? You were given Italy, and you spent weeks trying recipes until you found the one you believed to be most authentic. Will you make that for me?"

"Tonight, anything you wish for. I won't be able to make the pasta from scratch, but we'll make it work." He leaned over and kissed her on the forehead. He stopped next to Resa.

"What would you like? Your wish is my command."

"You cooking Italian. That sounds perfect to me. Thank you for everything."

"I didn't do anything but sit next to my sister as you two brought my niece into the world." He looked back at his sister. Propped up, holding Lorina, her long dark braid had fallen over her shoulder. "A world where strong beautiful women of faith will surround her."

Now Resa wanted to cry. Ana blinked and then looked down at her baby. "Your uncle is a poet. You must have brought that out of him."

Enzo whipped his gaze to her. "See how amazing she is already. Not even an hour old." He cleared his throat. "Well, I'll be in the kitchen if anyone needs me."

Resa watched him go. At that moment, she didn't think it would be possible to love anyone else ever again. It was over for her.

"He loves you," Ana said, pulling Resa's thoughts back into the room. She busied herself checking and double-checking everything, making sure all was clean and ready for the next steps.

"I know you heard me, so stop pretending to be too busy to respond."

"I know he loves me. He basically admitted it earlier today at my house, but it doesn't mean he'll do anything about it. I'm not doing this again. I wasted too many years waiting for someone to give me what I need. I am more self-aware now."

"But this is different." Ana pulled her daughter closer and studied the perfect little features.

"How? Because he's your brother?"

"Well, there is that. We would be real sisters. Our children would be cousins."

"He doesn't want children."

"That's what he said, but did you just see him? And then, the way he was watching you. I think he's changed his mind, and he wants you to be the mother of these children he suddenly wants."

Resa laughed. "If anything, he is more scared out of his mind. I know you mean well, but he's leaving. My life is here in Port Del Mar. Are you ready for a nap?"

Ana yawned. "Apparently, but I need to call Mom first. See if they have Julian."

Resa got her phone and they made the call.

Everyone was excited, but the rain was coming down harder, and many of the Houston roads were flooded. They were at the airport, and as soon as they picked up Julian, they would go to a hotel for the night. Her mom and Lorenzo wanted to come home, but her dad said it was too dangerous, and he wanted to be around to watch Lorina grow up. That put an end to the arguing.

They promised to call as soon as they got Julian to the hotel room.

"Now, give me that baby," Resa said. "I'll put her in the bassinet. You can reach her if you need to, but don't do anything if you're unsure. I'll be in the kitchen." She didn't put the little girl in the bassinet right away. There was something about holding a newborn that settled the worries of life.

"She's perfect, isn't she?"

"The most perfect baby I've ever met." Gently, she laid the sleeping infant down and stepped back. "Get some rest." She turned off the overhead light.

"And you enjoy your time in the kitchen with my big brother."

That's what made her nervous. Every time she was with Enzo, she fell a little bit more in love with him. That had to eventually hit a limit, didn't it? It wasn't possible to keep falling in love. "When did you stop falling in love with Julian?"

"That's an odd question." Ana thought for a moment. "When we first heard our little girl's heartbeat, he cried, and later, he laid his head on my belly to talk to her. Oh man. I fell hard on a whole new level. I suspect the minute I lay eyes on him, I'll drink in his details." Her gaze floated into a future scene. "If he has a bit of scruff on his chin or new lines around his eyes, I'll fall in love with those. My mom told me that one day last month, she came in from helping the kids in the orchard and found my dad with three little ones on his lap as he read a story. She said the best thing in the world is when your heart has new flutters over the man you've known most of your life. So, if she's right, I guess I won't ever stop."

That was Resa's fear. "You get some rest, but don't hesitate to call us." She gently closed the door and headed to the kitchen where the man who was probably the love of her life was making dinner for his sister.

No. She couldn't afford to think that way. There was too much life ahead of her to start giving up on love. If not Enzo, she would meet someone at the right time. Or not.

Either way, she had a great life and would make a point every day to be grateful.

Enzo closed the oven door and set the timer. It was the fastest he had ever made lasagna. It would be interesting, built with layers from leftovers he'd found in the fridge. There might be a little taco flavoring in the ground beef.

All he could think about was the new little

person who now shared the house with them. Holding Lorina had been life-altering.

He couldn't even imagine holding his own child. In the center of the kitchen, he closed his eyes. What would it be like? He immediately saw Resa, her hair loose and around her shoulders. She would glow after bringing the life of their child into the world. Her eyes would shine as she lay the bundle in his arms.

Every fiber in his being wanted that to be his reality. Was it too late? He knew she loved him, but could she trust him enough to let him love her?

His sister accused him of being in love with Resa since they were teens. The heavy weight in his gut told him she was right. Resa had scared him.

The sound of thunder shook the walls as a flash of lightning filled the room. That hit close. Then it all went dark. The storm surrounded the house.

Turning to the table, he popped on his lantern. The glow was strong enough to chase out the shadows. He had always loved a good storm. Being born on a day like this had to be good for a baby. Nothing would scare her.

Rain pelted the glass. Enzo tried to search the backyard to see if there had been damage to the main pole, but all he could see was darkness. There was not a hint of light past the window. He had left two lanterns in Ana's room. But Resa was afraid of the dark and might not find them.

He turned the corner into the hallway and bumped into Resa. She screamed.

The lantern fell as his hands gripped her arms to steady her. Her hand went to her chest. "You scared every bit of life out of me."

With a grin, he shook his head. "Impossible. You're overflowing with life."

"Resa?" Ana called from her room.

"I'm okay. Your brother was lurking in the hall, and I was startled. We're fine."

"Startled?" He realized Resa was still in his arms. She hadn't pulled back. "That was a scream worthy of the best overacting in a B-rated horror film." Taking a step closer, he loosened his hold on her arms.

To his surprise, she took a step closer to him and rested her forehead against the center of his chest. Holding his breath, he was afraid to move.

"My lungs have not recovered. Give me a minute. My heart is beating a mile a minute."

"Take all the time you need. I don't have anywhere else to be."

With a jerk, she pulled back. Apparently, he'd said the wrong thing.

"Don't you have to be in Colorado soon?"

Aw. He shrugged. "I have some paperwork to finish, but it can wait. Maybe I could do it from here and never leave again."

She took another step back. Her eyes had the look of a doe deciding if she was safe or should run.

Taking her hand, he picked up the lantern with the other. "I was going to check on Ana and Lorina."

"I went back in after we lost power. They have everything they need for now."

"Good. I have something I need to show you." Keeping her hand in his, he led her back to the kitchen. There was a soft rumble and, a few minutes later, lightning lit up the western sky. They paused at the bay window that faced her house. "I think it's moving on. We might see some sun after all."

"No matter how dark or long the storm is, eventually the sun can be counted on to clear the sky."

Studying their joined hands, he loved the way their fingers fit perfectly around each other. "Truer words have not been spoken. Come on." He took her to the back porch.

"What are we doing?"

He pulled a small box down from a shelf on the wall. "I have something I want to give you." He handed her a piece of folded rumpled paper.

She read the outside and then looked up at him with total confusion on her face. "This is the husband list they made me. Why are you giving it to me? I told you I'm done with this."

"Open it."

For a long minute, she stared at him, searching his eyes. Finally, she lowered her head and opened the page. Someone had scratched through each name. Then she covered her mouth and looked up.

"You crossed everyone else out and added your name at the bottom of the list?"

"Well, I would have put it at the top, but y'all didn't leave any room there."

She made a strangling sound that was trapped between a laugh and a cry. "You... you did this while you were making dinner?"

He shook his head. "No. I found the list over a week ago while I was looking for something. My feelings were still hurt that no one thought of me as an option for you."

"You know that's not true, right?" She waved the paper. "Our mothers and sisters plotted us being together as soon as they got you to agree to come to town. This was just to distract me."

"They played us?"

She nodded. "You hadn't figured that out yet?"

His eyes widened. "They did play us." Then he laughed. "They know me too well. They know me better than I know myself." He stepped forward and took her hand. "Teresa Espinoza, will you go on a first date with me?"

Tears welled up in her eyes. "What about the FBI? You're on a baby high right now. Let's settle down and take this slow."

"My whole life, I've taken things slow. I've been careful and followed the rules. Every decision and action was based on what I should do, never what I wanted."

"That's not a terrible thing. I've been impulsive and followed my heart when I should have thought about my choices more." Her grip tightened on his hand, encouraging him that she was hanging on despite her words of doubt. She wanted to believe in him, but he would have to earn her trust.

"I want to go in a new direction and explore options. The one thing I know without a doubt is you. I want to build a family with you. If that means adoption, having babies, or both. As long as it's with you."

"This is too much. You're scaring me."

"How?" His heart was pounding.

"You're handing me all my dreams in a perfect box. I'm having a tough time trusting it's real."

"There is nothing about me that is perfect, and you know that. Knowing all of me, you still love me. Let me love you."

She nodded. "Loving and staying are two different things."

"Fair enough." He got down on one knee and pulled her down so she was using his bent knee as a chair. "Resa, I love you with every piece of me, even the dark jagged ones. Will you date me, so that we can dream about, talk about, plan and put into action the future we want to build together?"

Cupping his face, she touched her forehead to his. "You want to know a secret?"

"If it works in my favor."

She chuckled. "I don't think I will ever tell you no when you ask so nicely."

His hands covered hers and he grinned. "Is that a yes?"

"Depends. Where are you taking me?"

"Easy. The Fall Festival."

"That's over two weeks away."

"You're the one who said we should take things slow. We already have breakfast and dinner together every day. I need to finish some paperwork and a few interviews over the last mission. That'll take a few days. It'll also let the adrenaline rush of being here for the birth of my niece fade." He quirked a brow. "You're the one worried about that, not me. I've been struggling and overthinking and overanalyzing these feelings for weeks. Today just hit me over the head about the time I'm wasting due to fear."

She nodded. "I'm done with fear too. I love you, and I'm not afraid to chase that."

"There will be no chasing. Just running toward each other."

"I like that." She leaned forward and placed her lips on his.

He savored the moment of being connected to her. Life was a beautiful mess, and God had brought him home at the perfect time to see the wonder in it all.

# *Epilogue*

One last look in the mirror made her smile. She had bought a special dress two weeks ago for this first date. A first date she hoped would be the last one. No more first dates. From now on, it would just be Enzo.

The dark teal skirt flowed as she twisted. Her hair was down, but she'd pushed it behind her ears and put on her wide-brimmed hat. There were three bold knocks on her door.

The butterflies in her stomach swirled in a mass migration. Why was she so nervous? He had been out of town, and she hadn't seen him in four days, but still…this was Enzo. She took a deep breath. What if he'd changed his mind once he'd spent time with the FBI?

Throwing her purse over her shoulder, she opened the door. Enzo was holding a large bouquet of brightly colored wildflowers.

"Hello." He shook his head. "You're gorgeous. These are yours. The wildflowers reminded me of you."

He sounded as nervous as she felt. They were both being silly.

"Thank you. You didn't need to bring me flowers."

"I wanted to make sure I start this off right. A first date is a special event."

She took the flowers and moved to the small kitchen. "Come in, and I'll put them in water."

He pulled out a notebook and wrote in it.

"What are you doing?" she asked.

"I had some help making a list of what to do on the perfect first date. I'm marking off the first two items."

"Seriously? Shouldn't we just have fun and go with the flow."

"We could, but then we might miss something. I want to make sure this is your best first date ever, because it will be the last one."

She laughed. "Okay. So what's next?"

"Well, the ones here in the middle can be done in any order." He grinned at her. "See. I can be spontaneous." He leaned over and kissed her. Pulling back, he whispered, "That was not on the list, but it should have been."

"Yes." She was a little breathless.

"It's a list full of apple picking, pumpkin-spiced drinks, and food. Carvings, hay rides and, um, a few other things."

"Sounds fun."

"Are you laughing at me?"

"Maybe." She wrapped her arm around his and pulled him out of her house. "Let's go have our date, Dr. Enzo."

"And that right there is the reason I never told anyone I completed my Ph.D last year."

She laughed. "But I love the idea of being married to a professor." He'd start his new job teaching at the college on the other side of the bridge next semester.

Hours later, they had done everything on his list, and a few unplanned ones. Her mouth hurt from smiling and talking. "This has been a rom-com dream date. I'm not sure I can walk another step."

"Nope." He was holding her hand as they strolled through the craft vendors. "Can't give in yet. There's one last thing on the list. We have to get our picture taken on the hay bales with the pumpkins."

She had created a monster. "Really, Enzo, you don't have to do this. You've proven your point. You know how to have fun, even if you use a list."

"Was that the point I was making?" He stopped and looked at her while taking another bite into his pumpkin empanada. It was from her sister's bakery.

Resa stood on her toes and draped her arms around his neck. "I love you. I'm exhausted. I never would have thought I would say this, but I am pumpkined out. I'm waving the white flag. Can we go to the tent and sit at a table like the old folks we are?"

"Hush. Even when you're eighty, you won't be old. Your heart's too young." He gave her a quick kiss that smelled and tasted of pumpkin spice. Okay, so she wasn't done with the fall flavor yet.

"Tía Resa! Tío Enzo!" His nephew was jumping and waving.

Enzo's whole family was sitting on the hay bales arranged at the entrance of the pumpkin field. "We're taking Lori's first family picture. Hurry. Momma says it's time to take her inside."

It took a few minutes to get everyone arranged. Resa stood on the back edge, next to Enzo. Julian pulled Princess Leia from his jacket. She wore a pink harness. "My son insisted that you would want her in the family picture." He handed the cat to Enzo, who was laughing.

The first picture was taken.

A few more followed. Resa had tried to step

out, but Enzo held her hand and handed her the cat. "You're both part of the family, now and forever."

Her heart skipped a few beats. This did seem like a forever kind of thing. Whether they got married the next year or in a decade, there would be no one else for her.

The family moved away. Her mother waved to her. When had her siblings joined them? It really was a family affair. This was the reason she loved living here.

It wasn't just special holidays but daily events they got to share together. She waved her mother over. "*Momi*, let's get a picture."

But her mother smiled and shook her head.

"It's your turn, Tía Resa." Lorenzo pulled her until she was sitting on the bale with the cat in her lap, then he ran off to stand between his parents. Everyone was in a semicircle around her and the camera woman. They all stood with the silliest grins on the faces she loved.

"Enzo, what's going on?"

He dropped to one knee in front of her. Heart pounding, she was afraid to hope. Her hands were buried in Leia's fur.

He held up a box. She couldn't focus. Was she crying?

"Teresa Espinoza. You are the light that chases away the darkness from my life. You are the joy that fills me with laughter. You are the wonder that proves to me that God loves us. Will you be my wife so we can share all the beautiful sunrises and darkest storms together?"

He was asking her. *Now. Today.* She glanced at the family surrounding them. They had known, and no one had let it slip.

Enzo Flores was on one knee in front of her as most of the town watched.

He cleared his throat. "Uh, Resa? Are you okay?"

They made eye contact and just stared at each other. One corner of her mouth went up.

"So I managed to surprise you? Is this a good surprise?" He rubbed his ear. "Is this too fast? I'm so sorry. I know we— Do we need to make this more private?"

She put two fingers on his lips and shook her head.

"Wait." He gently took her hand and pressed it against his beating heart. "Is that a 'no, I'm not moving too fast' or 'no, you don't want to be my wife'?"

Throat clogged with emotion, Resa didn't know what else to do, she leaned forward and kissed him. All the love and joy he'd spoken of poured out of her. She buried her fingers in his hair.

Cheering and hollering erupted all around them, but she didn't care. She was going to be Enzo's wife. He was going to be her husband.

He pulled back a little but kept their foreheads pressed against each other. The cat purred between them. "Just to be clear. You said yes."

She nodded and he kissed her again. A kiss that held the promise of a future she couldn't wait to live.

\* \* \* \* \*

Dear Reader,

Thank you for joining me on another trip to Port Del Mar. I love my Espinoza family. Enzo and Resa have a special place in my heart. They have been whispering their story in my ear for a very long time, and with the help of my editor, I've been able to flush it out and find all their hidden secrets.

After so many years of being seen as successful, Enzo wasn't sure how to deal with failure. For us writers, we get to guide our characters on their journeys, and at times we need their messages in our own lives. Dealing with failure and unmet expectations can be a challenge, but if we take the time to listen to God, we will know we are loved. We deserve to be loved and to love fully.

Enzo learned that lesson and it is a good reminder for us all. I pray you feel the love of God every day.

I love talking with readers. You can find me on Facebook at jolenenavarroauthor or email me at jolenenavarrowriter@gmail.com.

Blessings,
*Jolene Navarro*

# Get 3 FREE REWARDS!

## We'll send you 2 FREE Books plus a FREE Mystery Gift.

**FREE**
Value Over
**$20**

Both the **Love Inspired®** and **Love Inspired® Suspense** series feature compelling
novels filled with inspirational romance, faith, forgiveness and hope.

**YES!** Please send me 2 FREE novels from the Love Inspired or Love Inspired
Suspense series and my FREE gift (gift is worth about $10 retail). After receiving
them, if I don't wish to receive any more books, I can return the shipping statement
marked "cancel." If I don't cancel, I will receive 6 brand-new Love Inspired Larger-
Print books or Love Inspired Suspense Larger-Print books every month and be billed
just $6.49 each in the U.S. or $6.74 each in Canada. That is a savings of at least 16%
off the cover price. It's quite a bargain! Shipping and handling is just 50¢ per book
in the U.S. and $1.25 per book in Canada.* I understand that accepting the 2 free
books and gift places me under no obligation to buy anything. I can always return a
shipment and cancel at any time by calling the number below. The free books and
gift are mine to keep no matter what I decide.

Choose one:

☐ **Love Inspired**
**Larger-Print**
(122/322 BPA GRPA)

☐ **Love Inspired**
**Suspense**
**Larger-Print**
(107/307 BPA GRPA)

☐ **Or Try Both!**
(122/322 & 107/307
BPA GRRP)

Name (please print)

Address _____ Apt. #

City _____ State/Province _____ Zip/Postal Code

**Email:** Please check this box ☐ if you would like to receive newsletters and promotional emails from Harlequin Enterprises ULC and
its affiliates. You can unsubscribe anytime.

### Mail to the **Harlequin Reader Service:**
**IN U.S.A.:** P.O. Box 1341, Buffalo, NY 14240-8531
**IN CANADA:** P.O. Box 603, Fort Erie, Ontario L2A 5X3

**Want to try 2 free books from another series! Call 1-800-873-8635 or visit www.ReaderService.com.**

LIRLIS23

# Get 3 FREE REWARDS!

**We'll send you 2 FREE Books <u>plus</u> a FREE Mystery Gift.**

**FREE** Value Over **$20**

Both the **Harlequin® Special Edition** and **Harlequin® Heartwarming™** series feature compelling novels filled with stories of love and strength where the bonds of friendship, family and community unite.

**YES!** Please send me 2 FREE novels from the Harlequin Special Edition or Harlequin Heartwarming series and my FREE Gift (gift is worth about $10 retail). After receiving them, if I don't wish to receive any more books, I can return the shipping statement marked "cancel." If I don't cancel, I will receive 6 brand-new Harlequin Special Edition books every month and be billed just $5.49 each in the U.S. or $6.24 each in Canada, a savings of at least 12% off the cover price, or 4 brand-new Harlequin Heartwarming Larger-Print books every month and be billed just $6.24 each in the U.S. or $6.74 each in Canada, a savings of at least 19% off the cover price. It's quite a bargain! Shipping and handling is just 50¢ per book in the U.S. and $1.25 per book in Canada.* I understand that accepting the 2 free books and gift places me under no obligation to buy anything. I can always return a shipment and cancel at any time by calling the number below. The free books and gift are mine to keep no matter what I decide.

Choose one: ☐ **Harlequin Special Edition** (235/335 BPA GRMK)  ☐ **Harlequin Heartwarming Larger-Print** (161/361 BPA GRMK)  ☐ **Or Try Both!** (235/335 & 161/361 BPA GRPZ)

Name (please print)

Address _____ Apt. #

City _____ State/Province _____ Zip/Postal Code

**Email:** Please check this box ☐ if you would like to receive newsletters and promotional emails from Harlequin Enterprises ULC and its affiliates. You can unsubscribe anytime.

**Mail to the Harlequin Reader Service:**
**IN U.S.A.:** P.O. Box 1341, Buffalo, NY 14240-8531
**IN CANADA:** P.O. Box 603, Fort Erie, Ontario L2A 5X3

Want to try 2 free books from another series? Call 1-800-873-8635 or visit www.ReaderService.com.

*Terms and prices subject to change without notice. Prices do not include sales taxes, which will be charged (if applicable) based on your state or country of residence. Canadian residents will be charged applicable taxes. Offer not valid in Quebec. This offer is limited to one order per household. Books received may not be as shown. Not valid for current subscribers to the Harlequin Special Edition or Harlequin Heartwarming series. All orders subject to approval. Credit or debit balances in a customer's account(s) may be offset by any other outstanding balance owed by or to the customer. Please allow 4 to 6 weeks for delivery. Offer available while quantities last.

**Your Privacy**—Your information is being collected by Harlequin Enterprises ULC, operating as Harlequin Reader Service. For a complete summary of the information we collect, how we use this information and to whom it is disclosed, please visit our privacy notice located at corporate.harlequin.com/privacy-notice. From time to time we may also exchange your personal information with reputable third parties. If you wish to opt out of this sharing of your personal information, please visit readerservice.com/consumerschoice or call 1-800-873-8635. **Notice to California Residents**—Under California law, you have specific rights to control and access your data. For more information on these rights and how to exercise them, visit corporate.harlequin.com/california-privacy.

HSEHW23

### CARING FOR HER AMISH NEIGHBOR
*Amish of Prince Edward Island* • by Jo Ann Brown

When an accident leaves Juan Kuepfer blind, widow Annalise Overgard and her daughter, who is visually impaired, are the only ones who can help. He needs to learn how to live without his sight, but being around them brings up guilt and grief from the past. Together can they find forgiveness and happiness?

### HER HIDDEN AMISH CHILD
*Secret Amish Babies* • by Leigh Bale

Josiah Brenneman was heartbroken when his betrothed left town without a word. Now Faith Mast is back to sell her aunt's farm—with a *kind* in tow—and Josiah has questions. Why did she leave? Can he trust that she won't run away again? And who is the father of her child?

### TO PROTECT HIS BROTHER'S BABY
*Sundown Valley* • by Linda Goodnight

Pregnant with nowhere to go, Taylor Matheson takes refuge at her late husband's ranch. Then Wilder Littlefield shows up, claiming the ranch is his. He can't evict his brother's widow, so she can stay until the baby arrives—but soon they start to feel like family...

### THE COWBOY BARGAIN
*Lazy M Ranch* • by Tina Radcliffe

When Sam Morgan returns home from a business trip, he's stunned to discover his grandfather has rented the building Sam wanted to his former fiancée, Olivia Moretti. He's determined to keep his distance from the woman who broke his heart, but an Oklahoma twister changes his plans...

### A FAMILY TO FOSTER
by Laurel Blount

Single dad Patrick Callahan will do anything to help the foster kids in his care—including saving Hope Center, a local spot for children from disadvantaged backgrounds. When his ex-fiancée, Torey Bryant, is named codirector by her matchmaking mom, it could spell disaster...or a second chance at love.

### A FATHER FOR HER BOYS
by Danielle Grandinetti

Juggling a broken foot and guardianship of her nephews, Sofia Russo gladly takes a summer house-sitting gig out in the country. When they arrive, her boys are immediately taken with local landscaper Nathaniel Turner. And she can't help but feel something too. Could he be what they've been missing all along?

---

LICNM0723

# HARLEQUIN
## PLUS

Try the best multimedia subscription service for romance readers like you!

---

## Read, Watch and Play.

Experience the easiest way to get the romance content you crave.

Start your **FREE TRIAL** at
<u>www.harlequinplus.com/freetrial</u>.